D1282058

THE
RULES
OF
FATE

BY D.S. COOPER

THE
RULES
OF
FATE

D. S. COOPER

For Michael J. Maynard

"It was written I should be loyal to the nightmare of my choice."

Heart of Darkness
JOSEPH CONRAD

Saturday, May 5, 1945

The Tightrope Walker

"The war is over," the man said. "There is no need for any of your crew to die tonight."

"Do you wish to cancel your mission?" the captain asked, not looking at the man—rather, peering intently ahead into the fog and darkness.

"No, Captain. Now is the hour when I must succeed," the man said. "Do you wish for France to impose another Treaty of Versailles upon us? The Russians are barbarians. America is our only hope for better terms."

The captain and the man were standing on the conning tower of a Type IXC/40 U-boat of Nazi Germany's *Kriegsmarine*, creeping into shoal water through thick fog, blindly feeling for the boulder-strewn bottom until the keel ran aground close to a sandy beach. Then the crewmen began bringing six heavy cases up through the forward torpedo loading hatch to be stacked on the deck, each about the size of two shoeboxes.

"Take your nefarious cargo and leave my boat," the captain said as sailors launched a rubber dinghy from the bow.

"We should send a scouting party ashore first," the man said, "to be certain of our location."

1

"My copy of the American Coast Pilot contains highly accurate tide and current tables for this area," the captain said. "You will find yourself precisely at the spot you have specified."

"Thank you, *Herr Kapitan*. I pray for your safe voyage back to Lorient."

"No," the captain said. "I will gain better terms for Germany my own way, by entering Narragansett Bay and giving the Americans a taste of destruction in their homeland. Only then will they understand that German cities have already suffered enough from their bombs. Now take your cursed cargo and leave my boat forever."

The man came down from the conning tower and got into the inflatable boat with four sailors. Only two of the wooden cases were passed down to the raft, each requiring a duo of strong young sailors to make the transfer. Each case had black iron hinges, a stout padlock, and small loops of rope at both ends for lifting.

"Is it true?" one of the sailors asked as they paddled ashore. He was a tall, muscular machinist named Gunter Schmidt. "These small boxes must weigh 125 kilograms, at least. Are they the ingredients of a super-bomb? Will you avenge the Fatherland?"

"If that is what you want to believe," the man said.

"Yes, I believe you will make super-bombs in New York and Washington and other cities and destroy them one by one, until the Americans agree to a free Germany after the armistice."

"I will only tell you that my mission is to ensure a prosperous future for National Socialism," the man said. "The rest you will learn in time. But you, Gunter—you will be able to tell your grandchildren that you were here this night."

The raft rocked dangerously and nearly capsized through small surf but landed safely on a rocky beach beneath a tall clay cliff. The man carried the shovel and led the way up the steep terrain, arriving at a plateau of pastureland at the top where no lights or houses were to be seen. He quickly found a rubble-stone wall topped with a strand of barbed wire and said, "Here."

The sailors tossed the stones aside and Gunter began digging.

"You three go back to the U-boat for the other cases," the man said. "Bring them two at a time, with no delay. Time is now critical."

"How do you know so much about America?" Gunter said as he dug a deep hole into the clay and dry sand atop the bluff.

"I lived here as a child," the man said. "We used to summer on this very island when my father was a professor at Yale."

"What is that?"

"Yale is a great university," the man said. "It is not far from here in Connecticut. I lived there many years as a child."

In time the sailors returned with the other four cases and all six were lowered into the hole that Gunter had dug. Then the dirt and stone were piled on top and the grass in the area was smoothed to conceal their handiwork.

"Come, Gunter," one of the sailors said as they started down the cliff to the beach.

"*Viel Gluck*," Gunter said to the man, in parting. Good luck.

"Thank you, Gunter. You have been a good friend on the voyage. Now I pray for your safe return to Germany."

"Take this," Gunter said, detaching his Hitler Youth knife from his belt and presenting it to the man. "I would be proud to have you carry my blade into your lonely battle."

"No, Gunter, you don't understand—"

"You will carry my knife," Gunter said, pressing the blade in the man's hands. "Please."

Gunter turned abruptly and scrambled down the cliff before the man could return the knife, which he slipped into the inside pocket of his coat to be disposed of later, some distance from his landing spot. He stood on the cliff dressed in a shabby tweed suit with a raincoat and a fedora hat until he saw the shadowy form of the U-853 slip away into the night. He carried no luggage and he only vaguely knew that he was on the south side of the island when he started walking inland, carefully selecting landmarks so he could return to the spot. He passed small farmhouses where no lamps were lit and made his way from paths to lanes and then onto a gravel road, which he thought might be Cooneymus Road, so he went west toward the less populated side of the island, hoping to avoid the lights of the town of New Shoreham before he found the house where she would be waiting.

The horse and rider startled him when they came out of a side path, only twenty paces away.

The drowsy rider was hunched forward and appeared to be sleeping in the saddle. He was wearing a cracker-jack sailor suit with brown canvas leggings and a brown utility belt around his white jumper. There was a rifle slung across his back and he sat up and reached for it when the horse reacted to the man.

"Halt!" the rider said as his eyes opened wide. "Who goes there?"

"Hello, friend," the man said. "My name is John Potter and I am walking to a friend's house."

"At this hour? What friend? Where?"

"His name is Champlin, at Beacon Hill. We are going fishing at dawn."

"Half the people on this damn island are named Champlin and the rest are Dodges."

"Yes, I know many of them, as I have spent many summers here."

The horse sniffed evil and became restless when the man stepped nearer in the beam of the sailor's flashlight.

"Don't move. There are only two hundred people living on this island, and I've never seen you before. You will have to come to the Coast Guard station so we can sort this out."

"But why? I'm only walking to a friend's house."

"There are spies and saboteurs all around," the sailor said, awkwardly swinging the rifle off his back. "You could be a Nazi for all I know."

"Have you ever seen a Nazi?"

"No," the mounted sailor said, sitting nervously in the saddle and holding the rifle across his lap, with his flashlight in his left hand. "I've been stationed here on Block Island the whole war."

"Well, you could be right about spies," the man said, reaching into his coat. "Look, I found this knife near Old Harbor last week. It must have washed ashore from a sunken U-boat. You can have it as a souvenir to show your family back at home if you just let me go on my way."

When the beam of the sailor's flashlight caught the swastika on the knife, he jerked the bolt-action of his Springfield rifle open and closed, jacking a cartridge into the chamber. In doing so the young sailor dropped his flashlight and the horse spooked and reared so—in the inevitability of events in darkness and wartime—the rifle fired and the man who came in from the sea fell dead on Cooneymus Road with a bullet in his heart and a Hitler Youth knife at his side.

Sixty years later…

Saturday, May 7, 2005

Rendezvous

The passenger ferry *Metacomet* was a gallant sight—long and lean, built for speed and a smooth ride—when it slipped away from the dock at Point Judith and idled through the strong current in the breachway toward open water. The twin diesels sang a higher note in the Harbor of Refuge and the boat's high bow sliced through the steep chop near the west gap in the breakwater with ease. Morning fog lingered off Nebraska Shoals, but two radars turned above the wheelhouse probing the nineteen nautical miles of open water ahead, so the captain held a steady course to Block Island with the foghorn sounding at two-minute intervals like a lazy metronome giving the morning the *largo* rhythm of a bass drum beat.

The *Metacomet's* passenger deck was a clean and uncluttered space with benches and booths and a snack bar—like a bus station waiting room on a boat—where the crew held to a well-practiced routine that made you believe nothing remarkable would come to pass this day. Even so, Bennett and Natalie were primed for adventure when they took seats close to the bow with their surfboards and backpacks by their feet—bright, happy teenagers one month before high school graduation.

"I wish the boat would keep going past Block Island," Bennett said, "far out to sea."

"There's nothing out there," Natalie said.

"Everything is out there," Bennett said. "The whole world is out there."

"You sound like my reckless poet again," Natalie said. "Aren't you forgetting that you almost died in the surf at Ruggles six weeks ago?"

"Nobody ever died from a broken collarbone and a gash on their knee," he said.

"And a concussion," she said, her dark eyes probing for the truth in him. "You were out cold when Jeremy pulled you out of the water. Don't you remember how scared you were?"

"I never said I was afraid. And I wasn't blacked out, not totally, anyway. I saw what was going on underwater—I just couldn't do anything about it."

"But you were afraid," Natalie said. "Why won't you tell me? It's okay to admit you're afraid of what might happen. It might even be a good thing to say it out loud."

"I wish I could tell you, Nattie. I was never inside the curl of a wave before. It was like a giant spiral moving away, sucking me in like a tornado. I can't describe how awesome it was."

"That must have been terrifying."

"No, it wasn't scary at all—it was beautiful. The sun came through water above me like the stained glass of a cathedral, all blue and green and silver streaks—and time stopped. Why are so many dangerous things so beautiful? Thunderstorms and great white sharks, fast cars and jet airplanes?"

"Then you got stuffed into the rocks when the wave crashed down on you," Natalie said. "Tell me that wasn't terrifying."

"No, it wasn't," he said, his voice lowering to tell a secret. "The scary part was losing control. I was afraid I would panic when the curl of my wave closed in on me, Nattie. I felt fear rising in my throat like I was going to be sick and breathless at the same time, like my heart was stopping. I never want to lose control like that again."

"Rusty says that control is an illusion, Ben—that all skill is useless when fate calls your number."

"I guess, but I never thought it would happen to me."

"Well, the main thing is to get back into the water again," Natalie said. "And we'll be with Rusty Drake, so what could go wrong?"

The bluffs of Clay Head appeared through the mist, and the twin diesels became quiet when the *Metacomet* slipped behind the breakwater at Old Harbor. Then the motors suddenly roared in reverse to arrest the boat's headway and the captain spun his little ship around and backed into the slip, where crewmen tossed heavy mooring lines onto pilings.

"Where is Rusty?" Natalie said as they walked off the boat with their surfboards and backpacks. "He said he'd be here when the boat pulled in."

"Let's walk over to the newspaper office," Bennett said.

The *Block Island Times* was housed in a weathered-shingle building on Ocean Avenue with an American flag out front and a black sign with gold leaf lettering and scrollwork by the door.

"Nope, haven't seen him today," editor Leif Carlson said. "But that's not unusual, since we publish on Thursdays. I'm sure he'll be here Monday morning."

"He was supposed to meet us at the ferry," Natalie said. "We called his house, but there was no answer."

"Betsy is off the island today, isn't she?" Leif said. "Most of her photography work is on the mainland, you know. And if the surf's up, Rusty is probably in the zone and he might have lost track of time."

"I guess we could go find him," Bennett said. "Do you think Miss Hattie is around to give us a ride?"

"I'll call her now," Leif said, and her minivan pulled up in front of the office a few minutes later.

"Young man, you had a bad day last month, didn't you?" the notoriously nearsighted taxi driver said, when the pair was aboard her dilapidated island minivan with the broken taxi sign on the roof. Hattie's glasses were crooked and taped together and she wore an Orioles crewneck sweatshirt over yellow and brown plaid slacks.

"Sort of," Bennett said. "But it ended okay. I'm fine."

"Oh, Rusty was so upset!" Hattie said, demonstrating why the islanders claimed that her car was sound-powered and unable to move without a constant stream of words from her mouth. "But he wrote a beautiful feature that week. What did he call you, a *grom*, or a grommet? I don't know about surfing, but I get chills when he writes about that mystical bond between you wave riders, how you all share the joy of the surf and how you all feel it when another gets hurt. It's too bad he doesn't write about something good like true romance. He and Betsy had so many grand adventures, you know, when they traveled the world together. They didn't have any money back then, so they took odd jobs in all those exotic places so he could surf and she could shoot pictures. But no, he has to keep writing about surfing and fishing and all that ocean nonsense. I don't know why, but I suppose he likes that the ocean is all around us. There's nary a spot on this rock of an island where you can't see salt water, right? If you ask me, he should write about what goes on in the bedrooms when the summer people are out here—" Miss Hattie didn't miss a word as she threw the minivan with no suspension through the sharp curve on Harbor Hill where so many day-trippers on rented mopeds have cracked their bones—"It's true you know, Rusty is a direct descendant of Sir Francis Drake. Nelly Champlin says so, and she does the genealogy of every islander, and I guess Rusty and Betsy are islanders even though their grandparents weren't born here like the rest of us. Anyhow it's fascinating how many places we all came from to live here on this little island, back to the first settlers. Rusty has buccaneer blood but you wouldn't know it as calm and quiet as he is. I don't know if I know anybody as calm as him, just taking it in and writing about it all later. You can see it in his eyes when he sees and hears something to write about, like he knows something most of us don't. Oh, I love to read his features in the paper. He was a commercial fisherman when he first came here, you know, and hard winters on a boat do strange things to a man, you know, make him draw in on himself they say."

"This looks like the spot," Bennett said when they rounded the curve around the nature preserve at Rodmans Hollow. "How much, Miss Hattie?"

"Oh, three dollars, I suppose. You kids be careful now."

They walked the trail from the road to Rusty's favorite spot, where his old Ford "Woody" station wagon was parked in a small clearing between the thorny privets, scant feet from the edge of the high clay bluff above the rocky beach. His longboard was still on the roof rack.

"I don't know," Bennett said, when he stepped to the edge of the bluff with his own surfboard under one arm and his other palm above his brow to scan the water. "Do you see him?"

"Nope," Natalie said, the sea breeze ruffling her dark hair. "Maybe he worked the surf all the way around Black Rock Point, out of sight."

"Yup, the swells are setting that way. That must be why he didn't pick us up the ferry."

"Wait a minute," Natalie said, when they heard the sound of a cell phone ringing in the breeze. It was coming from inside the Woody. "Should we answer it?"

"Heck yes," Bennett said, and he opened the door and reached into the spartan interior. He loved the 1948 Ford Woody for the flathead V-8 engine and the big steering wheel and the long shifter coming out of the steering column—"three on the tree," Rusty had called it—and when he found the cell phone on the dashboard, he noticed that the keys were not in the ignition, which had to be a first for Rusty on an island where people seldom lock the front doors to their homes.

"Hello?" Bennett said when he got the phone to his ear.

"Oh?" Betsy said. "Who's this? Ben Laird?"

"Hi, Miss Betsy," Bennett said. "We heard Rusty's phone ringing in the Woody, so we answered it."

"Okay," she said. "Where are you, and where is my husband?"

"We're out by Rodmans Hollow, you know the place by Spar Point. Rusty must be surfing, because his longboard is here but his thruster board isn't on the roof."

"What? Didn't he pick you up at the ferry?"

"No, we got a ride out here from Miss Hattie and found his Woody. But—uh—we don't see him. He must have gone around the southwest side, or something."

"Ben, is anyone on the water right now?"

"Nope. Don't see anyone. Where are you, Miss Betsy?"

"I'm at the airport," Betsy said. "I just flew in from Westerly. Russell was supposed to pick me up, too. And he didn't answer his phone last night either."

"Uh—I'm sorry, Miss Betsy."

"Stay right there, Ben. I'm calling Rossi. We'll be right there."

Black Rock Road

Island cop Brian Rossi came along the trail from Cooneymus Road a few minutes later in his jeep with the blue light flashing and Betsy in the passenger seat.

"Can you see him?" Betsy said as soon as the jeep stopped. She was a slim woman with a curly auburn ponytail sticking out the back of a Red Sox baseball cap, still dressed in the khaki slacks and sweater she had worn on a commercial photo shoot on the mainland.

"No," Bennett said. "Maybe he's walking back along the beach."

"I hope he's okay," Natalie said.

"I hope so too," Betsy said, holding them both. She and Rusty had never had children, so they were still young at heart and fun for Bennett and Natalie to be with.

"I'm calling the Coast Guard," Rossi said. The island cop was dressed in his usual khaki shirt over dungarees with only a badge and a stainless-steel .357 magnum on his belt to identify him as a lawman. "And I'll get the fire department out here to walk the beach."

"We'll help," Bennett and Natalie said in unison.

"You two stay right here," Rossi said. "Did you touch anything in the Woody?"

"I just grabbed Rusty's cell phone," Bennett said. "It was ringing right after we got here when Miss Betsy called, but the battery is dead now, I think."

"I'll take that," Rossi said, and he placed the phone in his jeep while he radioed for backup from the Coast Guard and the New Shoreham Volunteer Fire Department.

When he came back to the Woody, Rossi said, "I see some loose straps on the roof. Is one of his surfboards missing?"

"Rusty usually lashed his thruster on top of his longboard," Bennett said.

"How long is a thruster?" Rossi said.

"About six feet."

"Let's sit over here where we can see the water," Betsy said, while

Rossi spoke into his radio. "But not too close to the edge. You never know when a piece is going to fall off this island."

"Right," Bennett said as they sat a respectful distance from the cliff with their surfboards and their backpacks. "There won't be much island left someday, the way these bluffs are falling into the sea."

"No kidding," Natalie said. "They'll have to move the Southeast Lighthouse back another three hundred feet."

"Actually, the island isn't shrinking as much as it's moving north," Betsy said. "Russell once wrote a humorous feature about a time in the future when North Reef stretched almost to Point Judith and the islanders were resisting the move with shovels and a bucket brigade of sand to the south side every night."

"I remember that fable," Natalie said. "They were passing buckets of sand across the island at night so the tourists wouldn't see. They didn't want to become part of the mainland."

"True," Betsy said. "If this wasn't an island, there would be no more islanders. Russell's point was that it would be a shame if they lost their identity."

"Rusty has a real way with words," Bennett said.

"Yes," Betsy said. "He certainly does."

Rossi was still focused on the Woody in the small clearing behind them when he said, "Betsy, since when does Rusty take his key out of the ignition?"

"Since never," she said. "Not in our island car."

"I didn't think so," Rossi said. Then he began looking in the grass around the Woody until he bent over about six feet from the driver's door and said, "Here it is."

He took a pen from his pocket and scooped up the silver ring with one key on it.

"Why did you pick the key up that way?" Betsy said. "He just had a senior moment and dropped it, probably."

"Sorry, sometimes I can't stop being a cop," Rossi said with a shrug. "I was twenty-five years on the job in Providence, you know."

"I know," Betsy said. "Don't let me bother you. This is a new experience for me. Do your thing."

"I don't mean to alarm you," Rossi said as he held up the key. "But the engine is stone cold, so it could have been parked here all night."

"Maybe Rusty slept in the Woody last night," Bennett said. "Surfers do that all the time."

"That's right," Natalie said. "Didn't you live in an old station wagon when you and Rusty cruised the California coast?"

"That was a long time ago," Betsy said. "But Russell calls me every night by nine o'clock when we're apart—except last night. And he didn't answer my calls this morning."

"Well, I'm not going to get any prints off this," Rossi said, putting the key on the dashboard of the Woody. "The key is still wet with dew, and so is the inside of this vehicle, since the windows were open last night."

"Rossi, what are you thinking?" Betsy said.

"You never know," he said. "There's nothing suspicious here, but my cop instincts tell me that something might get missed if I don't nail it down early on."

"Do you think some sort of crime is involved?"

"I doubt it. You'll be able to drive this vehicle home later, unless Rusty comes walking up the path with his surfboard any minute and asks what all the commotion is about. Like I say—you never know."

Betsy put her arms around Bennett and Natalie and looked out to the water, where a patrol boat from the Coast Guard station at New Harbor was cruising along the beach. A fire department boat came from the east side a few minutes later, and they soon saw a group of volunteers walking the beach.

"Things just got real," Bennett said when a gleaming white helicopter with a red racing stripe came whistling around Southeast Point fifty feet off the water and made a low pass along the shoreline with a crewman wearing a white helmet leaning out the open door. The big Coast Guard helicopter turned up the west side of the island and then came back, flying a pattern of sweeps over the water.

"How are you guys doing?"

"I'm afraid," Natalie said.

"So am I," Betsy said. "We'll just hope for the best. What are you thinking, Ben?"

"You mean besides worrying about Rusty?" he said. "I'm looking at that Coast Guard chopper. Those things keep coming into my life at key moments. Maybe that's where I should be."

Ebb Tide

Connor Laird was standing on the tarmac at Newport State Airport alongside a vintage twin-engine amphibious airplane with a grease gun in his hands, wearing paint-spattered khakis and a crewneck sweatshirt. On another day he might be wearing the uniform of an Anthem Airways Boeing 737 pilot, but even in the casual garb of his off-duty hours he still had the short hair—although it was now mostly gray—and the no-nonsense military demeanor of a long-ago Navy fighter pilot.

When his wife parked her Volvo and came through the fence toward the airplane, he said, "What's the big rush to get to Block Island?"

"It's Bennett and Natalie," Lorraine said. She had short sandy-blonde hair under one of the brimmed hats that she often wore to prevent the skin of her face from tanning, which might make the faint white scar on her left brow more obvious. "Rusty didn't show up to meet them at the ferry, and his car is at their favorite surfing spot—but he's nowhere to be found."

"I don't like the sound of that," Connor said. "Just give me a minute to finish greasing this landing gear."

"You should really give this contraption a new paint job before you carry any passengers," she said, looking at the newly acquired airplane with which he intended to start his own charter operation after he retired from the airline. "Seriously, the whole thing needs a total makeover before anybody will pay to fly in it."

"Peaches, do you have any idea what it would cost to paint this airplane? It's not like taking your car to Earl Scheib for a spray-over."

The airplane was a 1942 Grumman Widgeon, with long wings mounted atop a boat-like aluminum hull and a pair of six-cylinder Lycoming engines, each with 270 horsepower, turning three-blade constant-speed propellers. It had been built for the Navy and was sold as surplus to an oil company in Louisiana after the war. A doctor in Minnesota had used the Widgeon to take his buddies on weekend hunting and fishing expeditions for several decades after that, until Connor—like so many nearly retired airline pilots—had visions of being the proud owner of a prohibitively expensive and impossibly impractical classic aircraft. *If not now, when?*—the old pilots might all say.

"Can't you do something more permanent with this thing?" Lorraine said, when she tapped the outrigger float under the left wing. "I mean, are these little struts and wires the best way to hold an airplane together?"

"That's an elegant structure," Connor said as he wiped some grease off his hands. "It's designed to break away without destroying the wing if we hit something in the water. Now let's get going."

The Widgeon's passenger compartment was utilitarian, with four spartan seats behind the pilots, so Connor sent Lorraine to the copilot's seat on the right side of the cockpit while he pulled the boarding ladder aboard and locked the cabin door. Then he strapped himself into his seat on the left side and his hands began jabbing around the cockpit with the rapid but unrushed movements of a professional pilot preparing for flight.

Lorraine said, "Shouldn't you use a checklist?"

"It's up here," Connor said, pointing to his head between flipping switches and adjusting levers. "I've been doing this same drill for forty years—I think I can manage without reading a list."

"Yes, you are a creature of habit," Lorraine said. "Someday—just for one day—you ought to cut loose and not shave or shine your shoes in the morning."

"Yeah, sure," Connor groused before he grabbed the overhead throttle levers and put his head out the side window at his shoulder and said, "Clear!"

The engines coughed to life and quickly settled into a muted growl as Connor taxied to the runway, where he rocked the control wheel from side to side and fore and aft before he lined up on the centerline. "Here we go," he said to Lorraine as he eased the throttle levers forward and the engines sang a *fortissimo* tenor duet. As the airplane gathered speed, he pushed the yoke forward to get the tail-wheel off the ground and soon the Widgeon was arcing away from the airport and aiming toward Block Island, which was showing as a low smudge of brown on the blue of the watery horizon.

Connor managed a slight smile when Lorraine pulled out her Leica camera and took a picture of him in the act of flying the Widgeon. Here he was in his element, with the controls to a powerful airplane in his hands and a mission to perform. He was confident and relaxed, and in that moment she renewed her faith that they would survive the rough patches in their marriage—she had her own way of dealing with his random indiscretions—and that they would be together forever.

Their first meeting had been a dud, when Connor and her older brother Ransom were both graduating from Navy flight training in Pensacola while she was in her second year at Columbia. She had worn a peace sign to the graduation ceremony, which had infuriated Ransom but which Connor had considered to be hilarious. He had laughed at her all that day and treated her like a petulant child. "*What would a spoiled little rich girl know of the world?*" Which only inflamed her anger at Connor, the best friend who was leading her brother into what she considered to be an immoral war.

It was more of the same when she visited Ransom in San Diego before he left for the South China Sea aboard the aircraft carrier USS *Saratoga*. "Why does he have to be with us?" Lorraine said of Connor when they went to dinner. And she would someday come to regret her initial reaction when word came that a missile had gone past the canopy of Connor's jet and destroyed Ransom's airplane over North Vietnam. *Why did it have to be my brother? Why couldn't Connor have been shot down and imprisoned?*

Lorraine couldn't be there when her brother was released from the Hanoi Hilton—she was on assignment as a journalist in Central America at the time—but Connor was, and the photograph of the two wingmen reuniting on the tarmac of Hickam Field in Hawaii appeared in *Life* magazine.

Lorraine and Connor's meeting on a sidewalk in New York City a few years later was entirely by accident—if you believe in such coincidences. She was hailing a cab in front of Rockefeller Center when Connor came walking up Fifth Avenue in his Pan American Airways uniform—the scar on her left temple was new then, not long after the roadside ambush where the gunman held a pistol near her head and fired the shot that nearly lobotomized her—and she said, "Hi there, sailor, new in town?"

Their eyes met, and after a cup of coffee Connor took his best friend's kid sister to a hotel room off Broadway where years of pent-up passion exploded.

They had been together ever since.

"Landing gear down," Connor said out loud, and his words brought Lorraine back into the moment. They were flying over the bluffs on the south side of Block Island on a wide pattern to land at the airport. Looking out to the empty expanse of the ocean to the south, she knew that this truly was the edge of a vast wilderness of water. And she thought, *we'll never see Rusty again.*

Connor led the Widgeon through a sweeping turn over the Southeast Lighthouse and descended gracefully to the runway and then they were standing in front of the small terminal when Betsy drove up in the Woody with Bennett and Natalie.

"Thank you so much for coming over," Betsy said, sitting behind the wheel.

Connor said, "I could go back up and join the search from the air."

"The Coast Guard has that under control," Betsy said. "I'd rather you stay with me for a while."

"Sure," Lorraine said. "We can stay as long as you like."

"Then come home with me," Betsy said. "I haven't checked the house yet."

Connor and Lorraine climbed into the backseat with Natalie, and Betsy clunked the shifter into first gear and pulled away from the terminal.

"I can't help thinking that Russell may be there," Betsy said, when she drove up Center Road, leaning into the big steering wheel. "Maybe he got hurt and he walked home in a daze. He might be unconscious on the floor—"

Their house was a two-bedroom ranch on the west side of the island with an open living room and kitchen and floor-to-ceiling windows that offered a splendid view of Block Island Sound. One side wall in that main space had a small fireplace and shelves that ran full-span, filled with books.

"That's typical," Betsy said as she went around the house closing windows. "Russell left the windows wide open. It's an eternal struggle, I'm cold and he's hot, all the time."

"I could start a fire," Bennett said.

"That's a great idea," Betsy said, going to the refrigerator. "We probably don't have any food in the house. Russell is terrible about shopping when I'm away."

"Don't worry about us," Lorraine said. "I'll just make a pot of coffee, if you don't mind."

"Help yourselves," Betsy said. "I'm going to go out and look in the shed."

Natalie helped Lorraine with the coffee while Betsy went out the back door and opened the shed where Rusty kept his surfboards, fishing rods, and diving gear,

"I hate to see her this way," Natalie said. "It's so sad."

"Her husband is missing," Lorraine said. "Of course Rusty isn't out in the shed, but she's got to cling to any thread of hope."

When the islanders heard that Betsy was home, they began arriving with food and prayers. There were words meant to bolster her hopes—*as long as they haven't found his surfboard*—and words meant to soothe her—*everything happens for a reason.*

Lorraine went to Rusty's writing table near the bookcase while the neighbors ministered to Betsy. There was a large stack of paper next to his computer—his unfinished novel—and some other items that might be future columns or articles for the *Block Island Times*, or magazine articles. One collection of papers caught her eye for the handwritten note in the margin, *where is Cole Lonsdale now?*

Not long after sunset Rossi pulled up in front of the house and asked Bennett to come outside.

"Is this Rusty's?" the lawman said, training his flashlight on a surfboard in the back of his jeep.

"Yup," Bennett said. "Where did you find it?"

"The ferry spotted it halfway to Point Judith."

"Wow," Bennett's voice trailed off when he realized what that meant. "It must have been drifting for—a long time."

"Right."

When Rossi went into the house, he had to tell Betsy that they were calling off the search for the night.

"In the darkness—and with the fog rolling in—we can't do much more tonight. But we'll be back out there tomorrow."

"I understand," Betsy said. "Thank you. Thank everybody for me, please."

"Is there anything else you need tonight?" Rossi said.

"This might not be the best time to bring this up," Connor said. "But I have to get my airplane back to Newport before the fog sets in."

"I can give you a ride to the airport," Rossi said. "I'll wait outside."

"Fine," Connor said, "I'll be right with you."

"Oh, one more thing," Rossi said, on his way out the door. "We found Rusty's surfboard a few miles offshore. I have to hang on to it until this thing is over—that's state law—but I'll get it back to you as soon as I can."

Betsy said, "Thank you, Brian."

"Should I stay?" Lorraine said, after Rossi was outside.

"No, you should go home tonight," Betsy said. "The kids were going to stay with me and Russell tonight, so why not stick with that plan?"

"Are you sure?" Lorraine said.

"There's no one I'd like to have with me tonight more than these two," Betsy said. "We'll sit by the fire and talk about Russell half the night."

"We'll stay," Bennett and Natalie said in unison.

So then it was time to go and Betsy hugged Lorraine and said, "I wonder if I should tell Rossi about that other thing."

"It doesn't matter at this point," Lorraine said. "Maybe tomorrow."

Night Flight

B lock Island State Airport was a plateau of blue taxiway lights and white runway lights sitting atop the highest hill on the island as Connor and Lorraine took off and turned to the north.

"It looks like something out of a fairy tale," Lorraine said as he flew low over New Shoreham so that she could see the lights of the village rising out of a clear pocket in the mist before they climbed away into the dark sky. They both wore noise-cancelling intercom headsets so they could converse in normal tones, despite the engines roaring on either side of the cockpit.

"Connor, if I had known how sexy you look at the controls of an airplane, I would have flown with you more often."

"You've flown with me plenty of times."

"Not like this," Lorraine said. "On the airlines you were on the other side of a cockpit door. Seeing a man in his element up close and personal is something else."

"If you say so."

"You play this machine like a Stradivarius, tweaking this lever and that."

"I'm just synching the propellers," Connor said. "Don't you feel that pesky little vibration?"

"You make it look easy."

"It is easy," Connor said. "Anyway, what was that other thing Betsy mentioned when we were leaving?"

"Oh, that?" Lorraine said. "I don't think it's very important, now."

"So?"

"Russell had melanoma," Lorraine said. "He was diagnosed in November."

"I'll be damned," Connor said. "He looked fine when I saw him a few weeks ago."

"He was fine. They decided to put off the chemo as long as possible for a better—but shorter—quality of life."

"That's a tough call," Connor said. "But I would have played it the same way."

"You're so right about that. Betsy and Rusty wanted to stick to their routine as long as possible and just keep living their lives. That's what makes this doubly tragic—she lost those last sweet months with him."

"I wish he had told me," Connor said.

"That's the point," Lorraine said. "They didn't want Russell's end time to be heavy and morose. So many people mean well with their bromides and empathy, but the sorrow of others would just weigh a man like him down. He and Betsy wanted to keep it light and happy, the way they had always lived."

The Lycoming engines drummed in the night between their words, and the rotating green and white beacon of the island airport faded from view in the mist behind them. There was no land in sight ahead, but the lights of fishing boats and tugs with barges moved two thousand feet beneath the wings.

"What are you thinking, Fly-boy?"

"Mostly I'm thinking about finding Newport and landing this crate in one piece."

"Mostly? What else?"

"I'm troubled by what you just told me," Connor said. "I don't think Rusty would end his own life and leave Bennett and Natalie to find his Woody out there on the bluffs. Do you?"

"There it is," Lorraine said. "That's Betsy's nightmare—that people will believe that Russell was only thinking about himself."

"He would never do that to Bennett," Connor said. "No way."

"You're absolutely right about that," Lorraine said. "Rusty was one of the kindest and most considerate men I've known. He'd be thinking about others, right up to the end."

"Right," Connor said. "But our thinking can get fuzzy when mortality is creeping up on us."

"You've faced death, Fly-boy, and you're not all sappy about it."

"Sure, I've been in a jam or two, and so have you," Connor said, pointing to the faint scar on her temple. "Who doesn't laugh about dodging a bullet, when the sudden danger is past? Real courage is a long, slow duel with certain death and never flinching."

The lights of Beavertail Point and Castle Hill appeared slowly through the mist and then Connor began a gentle descent when the quilt-work of intersecting runway and taxiway lights of the airport came into view.

"There's no way Russell took his own life," Lorraine said as Connor dropped the left wing and entered a sweeping glide toward the runway at Newport. "He wanted to finish his novel. And he was working on something new—he had just started writing about that sunken Nazi submarine."

"The U-853?" Connor said, as he glided toward the runway center-line, holding a bit of power to slow the descent. "He'd already written a few articles about that wreck. And, I might add, when Rusty wrote about the ocean, he got it right, like the commercial fisherman he once was."

"This was some new angle on that sunken U-boat," Lorraine said as the wheels touched the pavement one by one and the airplane was down. "I saw his first draft, dated Thursday, and he was writing about some sailor or saboteur who came ashore the night before the Navy sank the U-boat."

"We're going to look into that, aren't we?" Connor said as he turned the Widgeon off the runway and retracted the flaps.

"Of course, Fly-boy. It's what we do."

2

Sunday, May 8, 2005

Bertram

"**D**ad, I don't like the thought of leaving you alone again today," Lorraine said to her father when they were eating breakfast in the large kitchen that spanned the back of the Laird house in Newport. The four-bedroom Victorian structure with a Mansard roof was separated from Catherine Street by well-trimmed hedges and an iron gate.

"I'll be fine," he said. "It's a beautiful morning to walk to Trinity Church for services."

In his eighty-sixth year, Ambassador Bertram Calhoun was a large man with closely trimmed white whiskers who had walked the corridors of power all over the world but who still possessed the pleasant Southern manners and flowing Charleston accent of his birth.

"That's a long way to walk on your own," Lorraine said. "Maybe Connor and I should delay our flight back to Block Island by a few hours."

"Definitely not," Bertram said. "You should be with your friends in their hour of need."

"Of course," Lorraine said. "I'll be staying with Betsy for a few days, but Bennett will be coming home with Connor tonight. I'm glad you'll be around to keep him company."

"I'm happy to be with you," Bertram said, "as long as I am needed here."

In fact, as of late the ambassador had spent very few days at his own large brick mansion on Tradd Street in Charleston—which had been in the Calhoun family for six generations—since he preferred the informality and relative anonymity of Newport to the demands of the Southern city where he was immersed in charity and politics. If very few Rhode Islanders recognized the former ambassador to Israel, India, and the Soviet Union when he walked down Thames Street, that was perfectly fine with him.

"I'll pray that you find your missing friend," Bertram said. "And later I'll look into that story about the U-boat he was working on. As I remember, there are some questions about that whole affair that have never been satisfactorily answered."

Tide of Secrets

Lorraine brought her Leica 35mm miniature camera and an overnight bag when Connor flew her back out to the island. A land breeze was pushing the fog out to sea when they arrived, so sea smoke was banked up a mile south of the bluffs like an offshore mesa of gray mist.

"Any word about Rusty?" the airport manager said as they deplaned. "It's a damn shame. Let me know if there's anything I can do."

They called Hattie for a ride to the Drake house—she squinted through her glasses and issued an unbroken stream of words of little import on the way—and when they arrived, Betsy was plating a pile of pancakes in front of Bennett and Natalie.

"This is round three," Bennett said as he stuffed a fork of pancake slathered in syrup into his mouth. "Miss Betsy is really spoiling us today."

"You're supposed to be helping," Connor said. "Not letting your host wait on you hand and foot."

"I love to spoil these two," Betsy said. "So, sit down yourselves. Coffee?"

"Sure," Connor said. "Just black, thanks."

"Did you get some sleep?" Lorraine said as she started cleaning the kitchen counter.

"Oh yes," Betsy said. "Truth is, the three of us fell asleep on the sofa in front of the fireplace. I'm not even sure what time that was."

Connor said, "Have you heard from Rossi this morning?"

"He called early just to say that they were out searching at first light."

"Betsy," Lorraine said. "If you don't mind, I'd like to write an article about Russell for the *Newport Daily News*."

"I don't mind at all. I welcome that idea."

"That's good," Lorraine said. "It also gives me an excuse to stay on the island tonight."

"I was hoping you would stay."

"Thank you," Lorraine said. "I should probably go talk to some of the residents on the south side of the island today while everything is fresh in their minds."

"Take the Woody," Betsy said. "The key is in it."

"Actually, Hattie is waiting out front. Why don't I leave Connor here and let her be my guide today?"

"Sure," Betsy said. "Hattie Wagner knows everything—or at least some version of everything—about everybody on the island. I'll see you later."

The morning was bright and chilly, and Lorraine wore a wool sweater when she went outside. Hattie was waiting in the old minivan and she said, "Where should we start?"

"When we flew in this morning, I noticed a few houses just west of Rodmans Hollow," Lorraine said. "The people there might have seen something, unless those are summer houses only."

"Oh no," Hattie said as she started the motor and drove away. "Those houses are lived in all year long. Do you know who lives there? You'll know him right away if he comes to the door, which he might not do since so many people just barge in to take a *selfie* or something silly like that. Nobody asks for autographs anymore, you know, they all want pictures with their cell phones. Dalton Montgomery is the vampire on that Netflix show, and he was the kissing killer in that movie with what's-her-name, the redhead one. Oh, he's a gorgeous man so I don't know why he always plays the evil characters because he is really a sweetheart and very polite and his family is very nice, even if they are quiet stay-at-home types. They homeschool you know. Three beautiful children and the two boys are identical twins. I can't tell them apart."

"Yes," Lorraine said. "I've met Dalton before, with Betsy and Rusty. Who lives in the other house?"

"Oh, the owner of that house is a big-shot moneybag from Boston, a banker or mutual fund tycoon or something, and I don't think he's been out to the island in years and years. A lot of the houses on the island are like that, the rich people build them and fill them with the most expensive furniture sent down from Boston or New York and then they hardly ever come and stay there for more than a few days. It's a waste, you know, but that's what the people with money do—they just leave it somewhere and forget about it."

"So nobody is living there now?" Lorraine said.

"Oh no. I didn't say that—the banker rents that place out. Not all the lawyers and doctors and bankers do that—those types own most of the houses on the island, you know, and they just leave their gorgeous homes empty all winter. But at least the banker has somebody living there."

"Do you know who he's renting to right now?" Lorraine said.

"Let me see," Hattie said, picking through a sheaf of disheveled notepapers rubber-banded to her sun visor. "His name is something Lawrence or Lawrence something, I think. Oh, here it is, Logan Lawrence. I think his girlfriend's name is Honey—that's what he calls her anyway. But she's never said a word to me, just looks down her nose with a lit cigarette in her hand and blows smoke my way like she's too good for the rest of us. Oh, we can go there next, but the Montgomery place is up this dirt road. Hang on because the hill is steep and there are lots of bumps."

Dalton Montgomery

Hattie left the pavement of Cooneymus Road where a small concrete obelisk like an old milepost marked the entrance to a narrow dirt trail that curved between thorny privets. There was a fork in the path about a quarter of a mile in and she turned the van to the right and drove another few hundred yards until they emerged onto a grassy clearing on the bluffs above the ocean. The house was a traditional cape with weathered shingles and a well-used Land Rover parked by the side door.

Hattie walked with Lorraine when she went onto the porch and knocked on the front door.

"Looks like nobody is home," Lorraine said when there was no answer.

"Oh, I wouldn't be surprised if they just aren't receiving visitors today," Hattie said. "Can't say that I blame them, with all the people wanting a piece of the vampire, you know."

"Well, maybe I'll try them another time," Lorraine said.

They were almost back in Hattie's van when a young family came hiking out of the bushy trailhead along the bluffs, with two boys leading the woman and a little girl riding piggy-back on the man's shoulders. Their shorts, smiles, and rosy complexions made them look like a page out of the LL Bean spring catalogue.

"Hello, hello," Dalton said, when they walked up to minivan. "How are you today, Miss Hattie?"

"Fine," she said. "I brought Betsy's friend Lorraine to see you."

"Of course, Lorraine," Dalton said. "We've spent a few pleasant evenings around Betsy and Rusty's firepit."

"Yes, in happier times," Lorraine said. "But I have to tell you up front that I'm here today as a reporter for the *Newport Daily News*."

"That's okay," he said, lowering his daughter to the ground. "Mia, why don't you take Miss Hattie over to your mother and brothers while Miss Lorraine and I talk?"

"I appreciate your candor," Dalton said after his daughter skipped across the yard with Hattie in tow. "Normally I don't talk to reporters and I'd appreciate it if you realize that this island is somewhat of a sanctuary for my family. As long as no one knows we live here, I can still walk down the street in New Shoreham with a bit of anonymity."

"Got it," Lorraine said. "My father was an ambassador so I understand completely."

"Thanks," he said. "Let's take a walk over to the bluffs. How is Betsy holding up?"

"She's a trooper," Lorraine said. "My son and his girlfriend stayed with her last night and this morning she was making way too many pancakes for them."

"That's good. She should be with people she loves and stay busy. We want to come by and see her but it's just too soon. Did she tell you that we had invited her and Rusty over for dinner next week?"

"No, but she's got a lot on her mind," Lorraine said. "Dalton, did you see anything unusual this weekend?"

"That's why I brought you out here," he said, standing near the grassy edge of the bluffs. "Our house is set back, so we can't see the beach and the surf from there, only the water a ways out."

"How about where Rusty's Woody was parked?"

"That would be a half a mile to the east," Dalton said, waving his hand. "We can't see a thing over there with all the brush and trees. Our first clue that something was amiss was when the Coast Guard helicopter flew by on their first pass, lower than the bluffs."

"It does look very peaceful out here," Lorraine said, pointing to a house closer to Rodmans Hollow. "How about your neighbor?"

"I can't say much about the fellow who is renting over there," Dalton said. "We haven't had much to do with him."

"I don't mean to be rude," Lorraine said. "But my reporter instinct tells me that this neighbor is not your kind of people."

"You might say that," Dalton said, with his most charming smile. "But I have an idea, Lorraine. Why don't you and Betsy come over for dinner?"

"I don't think Betsy wants to leave the house until—you know. And my son and his girlfriend are there, too."

"Bring the kids," Dalton said. "I'd like to see them again."

"Again?"

"Sure," he said. "Rusty brought them by once, and Bennett and Natalie threw the ball around with the twins while we had a cup of coffee. So the offer stands, whenever Betsy is ready and you are all out on the island, we'd love to have you over."

Logan Lawrence

Miss Hattie was uncharacteristically quiet when they drove to the next house. They had to go halfway back to Cooneymus Road and perform a sharp U-turn to go up the other fork in the trail, where an ultra-modern all-glass house with a flat roof sat perilously close to the bluffs, with a new BMW sedan out front, crusted in mud. On closer inspection, Lorraine saw that the expensive Bavarian automobile had New York license plates and that the fenders were scratched and dented from getting too close to the thorny privets and stone walls and farm fences along the trails.

Lorraine was still several paces from the house when a woman in a peach terrycloth jumpsuit threw the door open wide and said, "Whatever you're selling we don't want any."

"Hello," Lorraine said. "I'm Lorraine Calhoun Laird from the *Newport Daily News*. Can I ask you a few questions about the missing surfer?"

"We already told the cop we didn't see nothing," the woman said, exhaling a deep drag from her cigarette. "And the Coast Guard better stop flying that damn helicopter too close to our house and looking in the windows. There are laws against that."

"Is that a reporter?" a man prone on the sofa said. "Let her in, baby doll. And do the damn dishes, for craps' sake."

"Thanks," Lorraine said when she was in the house, where she saw the ocean through floor-to-ceiling windows and dirty dishes piled high in the sink. "I'd just like to ask what you saw yesterday."

"All I saw was a bunch of yokels breaking the law and violating my right to privacy," the man said. He appeared to be in his early thirties at most, wearing a white long-sleeve shirt and black dress slacks. His Gucci shoes—which were propped on the leather armrest of the sofa—had traces of mud on the soles and a rerun-of-a-rerun of a reality show about naked people in the wilderness was playing on the TV.

"Oh," Lorraine said, writing in her notebook as if his petty complaint was a significant fact. "What exactly did they do to you?"

"I'll tell you what they did," the young man said. "First they kept flying that damn military helicopter back and forth outside our windows. Do you know how loud those freaking things are?"

"That's right," Honey said. "And I was doing my yoga right out there on my own back deck, minding my own business, when they came by and gawked at me. Jeez! Like a bunch of grown men never saw a woman doing yoga in the nude before."

"Forget that," the man said. "Then the damn volunteer firemen came up here—on my property—and parked a truck where they could look down at the beach. They wouldn't even leave when I told them I was going to sue for trespassing."

"Okay," Lorraine said. "And your name is—?"

"I'm Logan Lawrence, Esquire—as in attorney-at-law. And I'm going to sue the shit out of all these local-yokels."

"I see," Lorraine said. "Is your law practice here on the island?"

"My practice is anyplace I sit my ass down," Logan said, holding up a cell phone. "But my main office is in the Millennium Tower in Boston."

"That's interesting," Lorraine said, continuing to scribble notes. "So, what do you think happened?"

"He had to be a damned idiot to be surfing alone at night," Logan said. "I don't see why they're wasting everybody's time trying to find a dead man."

Lorraine said, "You saw someone surfing at night?"

"No, that's just what someone said. His car was parked out there behind the bushes for a few nights, wasn't it?"

"And what makes you think he's dead?" Lorraine said.

"That guy was almost sixty, wasn't he?" Honey said, clanking and rattling what appeared to be fine china into the dishwasher. "The old bastard probably stroked out or had a heart attack and drowned."

"That's right," Logan said. "So what have you heard? Are they going to call off the search soon?"

"Well," Lorraine said. "Don't they usually try to find something before they give up?"

"He's shark bait," Honey said. "What's to find?"

Logan said, "How about his surfboard?"

"I believe they have found his board," Lorraine said.

"Well good," Logan said. "There it is—he fell off his board and drowned—end of story."

"Perhaps," Lorraine said, stepping around a black waterproof equipment case to reach the windows where a brass nautical telescope sat on a tripod. "You know, this is really a beautiful house. You have a great view from this little point of land."

"Yeah," Logan said. "It's for sale, if you're looking for a getaway place on the island."

"I don't know," Lorraine said, peering into the telescope, the optic of which was trained on a farmhouse farther along the bluffs, away from Rodmans Hollow and beyond Dalton Montgomery's home. "This place might fall into the ocean after the next big storm, the way these bluffs are eroding."

J. D. Dodge

"Who else lives here along the bluffs?" Lorraine said, as Miss Hattie drove away from the glass house.

"There are some nice houses down along Southwest Point," Hattie said. "I'll take you there."

"What about the farm past the Montgomery house?"

"Oh, that place?" Hattie said. "That's the Dodge pig farm. I don't think you want to go there—that's where you would find J.D. Dodge."

"So, who is he?"

"J.D. is only the most disagreeable old man on this island," Hattie said, regaining her nonstop talking rhythm as she turned onto Cooneymus Road. "Oh, don't think wrong of me for saying so but he is a miserable man. Old Cyrus Dodge started the island power company years ago and J.D.'s only grace is that he outlived all his brothers and sisters to inherit the company from Cyrus—that's how he got his money and control of so much of the island. If it wasn't for that, the town would have evicted him off that so-called farm years ago and made it part of the nature preserve, but J.D. is like a cockroach that you just can't get rid of. He's untouchable as long as he owns almost all of the stock in the power company. Until the wind farm comes, that is. When they build the big windmills off Southeast Point and put that electric cable to the mainland, J.D. will be done around here, that's for sure. I want to be there when they hold him down and shave off that stupid rat's nest of a beard—that's the ugliest thing I've ever seen—but he has no chin under there. That's right, nobody's seen what's under that rat's nest since he dropped out of the ninth grade, but they say he has what they call a receding chin and some people would like to hold him down and shave that stupid beard off and see what he really looks like, but J.D. always carries a pistol in his back pocket so that's why people just avoid him. I'd stay away from that farm if I were you—but this is the road to take if you really want to go up there."

"Sure," Lorraine said. "I might as well meet Mister Dodge."

"If you say so," Hattie said, turning the van up the dirt road to the farm. "Don't tell him I said so, but J.D. is just a skinny old man full of spite. He's just a wisp of a man, but that's not why he's small. Preacher Amos at the old Presbyterian church used to say that there's one big word that always describes a small man—belligerent. That's why J.D. is such a small man—he's just full of spite. But don't tell him I said so."

"Don't worry, Hattie," Lorraine said when she stopped the van near the farmhouse. "My lips are sealed. But before I meet J.D., would you tell me his first name?"

"Julian," Hattie said. "Julian Dolan Dodge, but don't call him that because J.D. hates to be called Julian."

"Well, I wonder if Julian is home," Lorraine said, when she looked at the house with missing shingles and the curtains in every window tightly closed. "This place looks abandoned."

"He's around somewhere," Hattie said. "That's his Cadillac—nobody else would have a big old green El Dorado—and he only drives the dump truck to take junk off the island once a month, maybe. So he's hereabouts, I'd say."

Lorraine was only a few steps away from Hattie's van when a John Deere tractor came driving toward her at high speed. The driver swerved at the last moment to avoid cutting her in half with the front bucket and stopped the machine directly in her path, halting any advance toward the farmhouse.

"Can I help you?" the driver said with a crooked-tooth sneer. He was sitting high in the tractor's saddle and speaking loud enough to be heard over the rattling and rumbling of the motor.

"You must be J.D. Dodge," Lorraine said, seeing the untamed gray whiskers tangled below his face. "I'm Lorraine Calhoun Laird from the *Newport Daily News*. Can I have a few words with you?"

"About what? You better not be bothering me about that wind farm because I'm telling you right now, it ain't never going to get built—never."

"No, I'd like to ask just a few questions about the missing surfer," Lorraine said. "You must know about everything that happens on this island."

When J.D. shut off the tractor's motor and stepped down, Lorraine found herself facing a remarkably skinny man in a dirty sweatshirt and dungarees that somehow stayed up even though his belt had no apparent waistline or hips to cling to.

"What about the surfer?" he said, standing like a crooked tree with his arms crossed over his chest.

"I'm wondering if you saw anything," Lorraine said.

"Nope," he said. "I don't recall nothing special." Then J.D. raised his right hand to stroke his beard and said, "What do you hear about it?"

"It's still a mystery," Lorraine said, thinking that petting his beard might be a thoughtful gesture—or that it may be a reflex action to shield his nonexistent chin behind the beard. "There are lots of theories, but nobody really knows what happened to Rusty Drake."

"What are people saying?" J.D. said, still standing crooked with his arms crossed over his skinny chest.

"Well, they found his surfboard a long way from where his Woody station wagon was parked," Lorraine said. "But nobody really knows when he first went into the water or where he is now."

"How about that cop Rossi—what does he think?"

"I haven't had a chance to talk to him," Lorraine said. "Right now, Chief Rossi is totally occupied with the search and rescue effort."

"Well, I tell you what," J.D. said, turning his head to spit tobacco juice. "You come back and talk to me after Rossi calls off this stupid search for a dead man and I might have something
to say."

Then he climbed back onto the tractor and said, "You might give Rossi some advice too—the islanders don't need no outsider nosing around where he ain't got no business. Island cops come and go—so he ought to just keep the tourists in line and leave us alone."

Tony Marino

"We're out of milk," Natalie said when she opened Betsy's refrigerator.

"I know," Betsy said. "Even with all the food my neighbors brought I'm still running low on a few things, but to tell the truth I'm just not ready to go into town yet."

"Let us take care of your shopping," Connor said. "We'll take the Woody to the grocery store. What else do you need?"

Betsy put together a quick list and then Connor drove Natalie and Bennett into New Shoreham, where the residents all recognized Rusty's Woody and had to say a few well-meaning words.

"I see why Betsy wasn't ready to come into town," Bennett said, after twenty or so people asked for the latest news and offered sappy condolences.

"She just needs a little time," Natalie said.

"You know what I hate?" Bennett said as he pushed a shopping cart through the island grocery while Natalie and Connor picked items off the shelves.

"Hate is a strong word," Connor said.

"Okay then," Bennett said. "Do you know what I don't like? I don't like when people say stuff like 'everything happens for a reason.' How is that supposed to make Betsy feel better?"

"Those are nice people," Natalie said. "They're just trying to make some sense out of a tragedy."

"Some people think there's a grand plan to life," Connor said as he tossed a box of pasta into the cart.

"What do you think?" Bennett said.

"I take it one day at a time," Connor said.

They checked out with far more items than Betsy had requested, and when Connor opened the back door of the Woody, he said, "Looks like the groceries are going on the backseat. There's no room here with all Rusty's gear."

"I guess I should put all this fishing and diving stuff in the shed when we get back to the house," Bennett said.

"Look who's pulling into Old Harbor," Connor said as he looked to seaward. "That's Tony Marino's boat—the *Racketeer*."

"It sure is," Bennett said. "Doesn't he run charters out of Newport? I wonder what he's doing out here."

"Let's go down to the dock and ask him," Natalie said.

"Natalie, you're a girl after my own heart," Connor said.

"I know," Natalie said. "Any excuse to go look at boats, right?"

Connor drove onto the pier in front of Ballard's restaurant as Tony's boat idled in through the breakwater. The *Racketeer* was a beamy fiberglass vessel, forty-two feet long with a wide-open deck behind a spacious pilothouse that contained the steering station and a simple galley.

Tony was twenty feet off the dock when he gave the engine a quick shot of reverse to kill his headway, which also kicked the boat's stern to port. Then he stepped away from the helm and picked up his mooring lines while the boat coasted sideways precisely to his spot, where he handed the bow and stern lines to the teenagers, who cleated the ropes with the speed and precision that comes naturally to those who have grown up near the ocean.

"Captain, I really enjoy watching you drive a boat," Connor said. "That landing was a piece of art."

"Thanks," Tony said, looking up from the deck with a laugh. Then like all true masters of any craft, he modestly added, "Sometimes it works out nice and sometimes it don't. You wouldn't want to see when it don't—it can get pretty ugly."

"Right," Connor said. "What brings you out to Block Island on a Sunday afternoon, Tony?"

"I was going to ask you the same thing," Tony said, scratching the beard that connected his sideburns by way of his chin. The curly wreath of hair around the bald crown of his head and his thick forearms on a stocky frame completed the image of what a sailor should look like.

"Unfortunately, that missing surfer is a friend of ours," Connor said. "You probably know him, too—Rusty Drake."

"Oh no," Tony said. "That was Rusty? Oh for crap's sake, that's a damn shame because he was one hell of a nice guy and a damn good writer, too. And he paid his dues on the water, that's for sure. Nobody writes about the ocean like a real commercial fisherman."

"I'll pass that on to Betsy," Connor said.

"You do that," Tony said. "I'm only out here because some guys from New York want to dive on the submarine to make a movie for The History Channel or something and they chartered me for a whole week. They're bringing their gear aboard today so we can get started first thing tomorrow."

"The U-853?" Connor said. "I guess it is okay to film as long as they respect the sailors who died on that boat. They're still out there in a watery grave, Tony. I really don't like to see pictures of human skulls and bones that have been propped up for effect."

"I know," Tony said. "I made them swear to show some class before I agreed to this charter. I think they're going to be okay because they seem to be interested in serious maritime history, not some cheap video."

"In that case it sounds like the charter is a good deal for you, Tony. Anything we can do for you while we're here?"

"No, I'm all set, thanks. I got everything I need right onboard, so I'll be sleeping in the cabin."

The ferry *Metacomet* had pulled into Old Harbor and backed into the slip to offload while Connor and the teenagers were talking to Tony. They watched as the crewmen guided several cars off without incident until a black Humvee disregarded the sailors' signals and scraped against the bulwark as it was driving off the boat, too fast.

"I wonder what the big rush is?" Bennett said as they climbed into the Woody.

"I don't know," Natalie said. "But I bet the owner of that black Humvee is going to be ticked when he notices the big gash of white paint from the ferry on his car."

"He'll blame the ferry crew," Connor said. "It's always somebody else's fault."

They arrived back at the Drake house a short time later, where Connor and Natalie took the groceries in while Bennett opened the back of the Woody and took Rusty's gear into the shed. He carried the fishing gear first and hung the rods from the hooks in the shed's rafters. Then he brought in the diving equipment before he went back to the Woody for another wetsuit, which had been under the other stuff.

When he came into the house through the kitchen door, Bennett said, "When did Rusty get a new wetsuit?"

"He's already got three," Betsy said. "Why would he need another?"

"Gee, I don't know, Miss Betsy," Bennett said. "But all three of his wetsuits are hanging in the shed now, and so is his diving dry suit. So—"

The Professionals

Betsy finally agreed to allow Bennett and Natalie to prepare a meal for her, so she sat in the living room near the big windows overlooking Block Island Sound with Connor and Lorraine while the teens busied themselves in the kitchen.

"I can't make any sense of Rusty's wetsuit being in the Woody," Connor said. "The ocean water temperature is about forty-five degrees this time of year, so he would have to wear a wetsuit to survive. Unless—"

"You don't have to say it," Lorraine said. "We're all thinking about that."

"Thinking about what?" Bennett said as he came out of the kitchen to refill their coffee cups.

"Nothing you need to worry about," Connor said.

"No," Betsy said. "It's about time they should know. Come over here, Natalie."

Betsy sat the teenagers down on the sofa and said, "Russell had cancer."

"What?" Bennett said.

"Ben, he didn't want anyone to know," Betsy said. "I hope you'll understand why we didn't tell you. It was melanoma—a very bad case. We didn't have long—"

"I don't believe it," Bennett said.

"I'm so sorry," Natalie said, holding Betsy's hand.

"That's not what happened," Bennett said, jumping to his feet. "We were going surfing. He was supposed to pick us up at the ferry. That's not what happened."

Connor said, "Rusty knew how quickly hypothermia would overtake him without a wetsuit, Ben. They say it's not a bad way to go."

"I don't believe it," Bennett said, moving to the windows where he looked out to the water. "You're wrong. Rusty wouldn't do that."

Connor set his jaw in silence and looked at his son's back while Lorraine moved to the sofa to comfort Betsy. Then Natalie stood up and said, "Come on, Ben. We have to finish preparing dinner."

"I don't believe it," Bennett said, very softly. Then he wiped tears from his eyes before he turned from the window and rejoined Natalie in the kitchen.

Lorraine and Betsy were leaning against each other on the sofa when Connor said, "Tell the truth, I don't believe it either."

"None of us want to believe it," Lorraine said.

"It doesn't make any sense," Connor said. "Rusty always leaned forward into life. He wouldn't give up a single day while he still had the strength to get out of bed and do something—anything—and if it was something challenging and a little dangerous, that was all the better for him."

"That's a fact," Betsy said. "The only time Russell sat still was when he was writing, and even then he would sometimes pace around the

room muttering like a lunatic while he tried to work out the exact words
to use."

"Right," Connor said. "I think we can just discard the idea that he
ended his own life."

"But what does that leave us with?" Lorraine said.

"Just maybe," Betsy said, "Russell is somewhere on the island. He
could be hurt and lying in the bushes for all we know."

"That's a long shot," Connor said. "The main thing we have to do is
to tell Rossi about the wetsuit. The searchers have been hoping that if
Rusty was wearing a wetsuit it might give him buoyancy and some
protection from the cold water. This changes all that."

"I'll call him right now," Betsy said.

Later, after they finished the meal that Natalie and Bennett had
prepared and the dishes were done, Connor said, "We should shove off
soon."

"Yes," Lorraine said. Then she turned to the teenagers and said,
"Why don't you two get your things together, and I'll take you to the
airport in the Woody."

"Can't we just skip school for a few days?" Bennett said.

To which Connor said, "Get moving, Ben."

Betsy's good-byes with the teens was a little longer and more emo-
tional than usual, but she eventually let them go with promises to return
the next weekend. Then there was a quiet ride to the airport where
Lorraine dropped them off in front of the terminal, after which she
headed back to spend the night with Betsy.

"Look who that is," Bennett said when the homeward-bound trio
came out through the airside of the terminal building and saw a black
Humvee alongside a turboprop airplane, complete with the white slash
of paint from the ferry on the side.

"I'll be darned," Connor said. The turboprop—which had apparently
just landed—was parked alongside the Widgeon, and a uniformed pilot
was helping his two passengers remove a large pile of equipment from
the airplane to be loaded into the Hummer.

"That looks like diving gear," Natalie said. "Do you suppose that's
Tony's crew?"

"Could be," Connor said as they walked to the Widgeon. Then when they were passing by the turboprop close enough to speak with the men he said, "That's some fancy gear you've got there."

One of the young men said, "We're professionals," as he loaded a metal detector into the Humvee.

"That's interesting," Connor said. "I don't suppose you're going to dive on the U-853?"

"If we feel like it." The Humvee driver shrugged.

"What's the metal detector for?" Connor said. "Don't you know that the wreck has been picked clean by generations of sport divers? It's one of the most popular dive sites in New England."

"We know what we're doing," another man said. The two young men who had arrived by airplane and the driver of the Humvee were all dressed in the style of high-end expedition clothing that an affluent city-dweller might wear in an effort to appear adventurous. "Isn't that right, Dirk?"

"True that," said the one named Dirk.

"I'm sure you do," Connor said, looking at a set of hydraulic shears being loaded into the Humvee. "But you seem to have some equipment to tear the wreck apart, which you're not supposed to do."

"Says who?" one of the men said.

"Says the government of the United States and the Government of Germany. The U-853 is a protected war monument. You can look all you want, but you can't disturb the wreckage or dig around in the mud for souvenirs."

"Why don't you mind your own business?" Dirk said.

"It is my business," Connor said. "If any of you were veterans, you'd understand why. I expect the remains of my comrades left behind in North Vietnam to be treated with respect, and I honor the combatants of all nations when the fighting ends."

"Ha!" One of the men laughed and then the others joined in. "Are you kidding? Nobody has time for that crap anymore."

"You lost your ass in Vietnam and nobody really cares anyway," Dirk said. "Get over it, old man."

Connor forced a smile and unclenched his fists when he said, "Let's go," to Bennett and Natalie.

When they were climbing aboard the Widgeon, Bennett said, "You don't like those guys, do you, Dad?"

"Nope, I don't care for them at all," Connor said.

"Why didn't you punch that guy named Dirk in the nose?"

"Just forget about Dirk and his buddies, Ben. Go ahead and hop into the copilot's seat. Do you think you could get these engines started, with a little help from me?"

"Sure, just tell me what to do."

This time Connor had Bennett read from the checklist and soon the engines were idling and Connor was taxiing the Widgeon to the runway, where he said, "Follow me through on the controls."

Connor pushed the throttles on the ceiling ahead and engines roared as they trundled down the runway and rose into the sky. Then he took his hands off the controls and allowed Bennett to aim the airplane toward Point Judith, insisting that he hold the proper heading and altitude with minor corrections.

"Don't ask a bunch of questions," Connor said. "Just watch—and do what I tell you to do—and you'll figure it out on your own. Someday, if you decide you really want to fly, we'll get you an instructor to fill in the blanks."

Connor took the controls again when they were over Point Judith, where he circled the Harbor of Refuge and then came in over the lighthouse. He reminded himself several times *not* to put the landing gear down before the Widgeon's hull began skipping over the wavelets on the surface of the water. Loud slaps reverberated through the airframe until they settled deeper as he eased the throttles back—until they were almost stopped and the airplane's nose settled hard into the water, sending a plume of heavy spray over the engines and wings.

"Congratulations," Connor said. "You just survived your first water landing."

"Was all that splashing normal?" Natalie said.

"Happens every time," Connor said. "That's why we have to douse this airplane with fresh water after every ocean landing."

He maneuvered the amphibian close to the beach and spun it around, letting Bennett and Natalie jump off in waist-deep water while the

Widgeon glided slowly away with the engines idling, in full view of some astonished diners at George's of Galilee. Connor left his seat briefly to secure the boarding hatch while the teenagers waded ashore. Then he gunned the engines and took off to the west, easily clearing the boulders of the breakwater surrounding the harbor before he pivoted around the lighthouse on Point Judith and flew toward Newport, where the afternoon sun was casting long shadows over the ruins of the concrete fortifications that had once guarded the entrance to Narragansett Bay.

3

Monday, May 9, 2005

Too Soon

Lorraine woke up early and looked out the big windows at Block Island Sound while the coffee was brewing and Betsy was still sleeping. Then she took a cup and sat down at Rusty's little writing table in the living room where there was just room for his notebook computer with the large stack of paper that was to be his novel on one side and some smaller projects on the other. His reporter's notebook was on top of the smaller pile of papers, so she opened that first and scanned through it. Most of the notes were in scribbled cursive—almost a form of shorthand—so they had probably been jotted down during interviews. But he always printed names and dates in block letters to be certain of the spelling and accuracy, and one such entry piqued her curiosity—Cole Lonsdale, Pawtucket RI.

When Lorraine sifted through the smaller stack of papers, she saw the name Cole Lonsdale again penciled in the margin of an article Rusty had written as if it was an afterthought, with an arrow pointing to the name Gunter Schmidt and the date of May 5, 1945 in the text.

The last entry in Rusty's notebook was one printed name with a question mark—Laura Ingalls?—which Lorraine discounted since the famous author of the frontier life books didn't connect to the U-boat and was probably the start of another story.

The sun was up when Betsy emerged from her bedroom and said, "That coffee smells great."

"Good morning," Lorraine said. "Did you have a good sleep?"

"Actually I did," Betsy said, as she sat on the sofa with a cup. "I woke up around three but managed to fall back under. Are you finding anything interesting in Russell's writing?"

"I hope you don't mind," Lorraine said. "I was just curious about what he was working on."

"He was always working on that damn novel," Betsy said. "Did you read any of that?"

"Not today," Lorraine said, getting up from Rusty's desk to refill her coffee cup. "I was picking through his notebook and these articles."

"I suppose I'll have to read the whole book eventually," Betsy said. "But it's a little too soon for me."

"I know," Lorraine said, sitting next to Betsy on the sofa. "When I read him, I can hear his voice as if he's speaking the words out loud to me. He is such a great writer."

"Yes, he certainly was good at his craft," Betsy said. Then she looked directly at Lorraine and said, "Oh my God, did I just mention Russell in the past tense?"

"Yes, you did."

"That was the first time," Betsy said. "But it is true, isn't it? I've lost him."

"I think so."

For a time Betsy looked into her coffee cup as if the answer were in there and then she raised her eyes to the windows and the salt water beyond and said, "I wonder if I'll ever get him back. You know, his—"

"Perhaps," Lorraine said.

"In a way I hope the sea never gives him up," Betsy said. "I can always look out at the water and know he's there on the ocean he loved."

"He certainly did love the ocean," Lorraine said. "Almost as much as he loved you."

"Thirty-two years," Betsy said. "We met on Patriots' Day in Boston in 1973 and never let go of each other—I should be crying but I can't. I just feel empty and alone. I don't know what I'll do from here, Lorraine. I don't know what step to take next—when will I—"

"I don't think we ever get over it," Lorraine said. "You just try to get through this cup of coffee and then the next. Then you face the morning and then the afternoon and another night. You just take it one step at a time and learn how to move on, but the emptiness never goes away and you'll miss him forever—time never heals that—you just learn how to live with it until only the good memories remain."

"Spoken like a writer," Betsy said. "Did you pen those lines in one of your books?"

"Well, yes," Lorraine said, with a shrug. "I did, but they work here, too."

"Great," Betsy said, half-sobbing and almost laughing in the same breath. "Recycled wisdom is better than none, I guess."

"That's all I've got," Lorraine said.

"Thanks," Betsy said. "Now I've got to get up and do something. This house is a mess and there's a pile of laundry to be done."

"I'll help," Lorraine said.

"You know what you could do for me today?" Betsy said. "You could take the Woody to the *Times* and speak with Leif Carlson. Russell must have some unfinished business with the newspaper, and you're the one to look after that."

The Times

"We're all in shock," editor Leif Carlson said when Lorraine walked into the office of the *Block Island Times*. "Nobody expected this. How is Betsy?"

"She's dealing with it," Lorraine said. "I think that shock is the right word."

"If there's anything I can do—"

"That's why I'm here," Lorraine said. "You can help me finalize some of Rusty's writing. I did come across what looks like the working draft of a magazine article on his writing table, and it would help Betsy emotionally and financially if I can polish that up and get it published posthumously."

"How about his novel?" Leif said. "It would be a shame if that was lost."

"I'm not sure," Lorraine said. "Rusty let me read parts of the first draft over the past few years and it is absolutely dynamite. But I'm not sure I could do it justice—I'm simply not as good a writer as he was."

"No offense, but I have to agree," Leif said. "Rusty poured honey on the pages—the prose in his nonfiction books is a pure delight to read, even if you have no interest in the ocean. Authors like that only come along once in a decade so it would be a tragedy if that novel never gets published."

"You're right, but that's for another day," Lorraine said. "Today I'm interested in this article he was writing about the U-boat sunk near here in 1945."

"I'm not surprised," Leif said. "This is the sixtieth anniversary of that, almost to the day. In fact, he had pulled some microfiche plates of old editions from our library. I think they're still on his desk."

"May I?" Lorraine said, and with a nod from Leif she leaned over Rusty's desk, where there were two small protective folders holding the miniature photographic copies of the *Block Island Times* from September 1944 and May 1945. She took folders to the back of the office and put the one from September in the viewer first, and moved the tray to scroll through the pages. The paper's masthead had the identical vintage calligraphy and scrollwork of the current issue, along with the motto, *Block Island's Hometown Newspaper.*

September's headlines were not all about the war although one column of print was dedicated to Captain Eugene Dodge, who reported that—

A U-Boat surfaced near his trawler in the early morning hours of Tuesday previous and demanded milk and bread. Captain Dodge complied and added a pound of baloney a bottle of blackberry brandy from his provisions to be graciously received by the commander of the submarine, which forthwith vanished into a fogbank.

The article also noted that Captain Dodge was unable to notify the Coast Guard of the U-boat's proximity to the island due to a faulty radio, which had since been repaired.

A much larger story was the arrival of a hurricane on September 14, which sank a Navy destroyer and two Coast Guard cutters near Cape Hatteras with great loss of life, but which miraculously diminished as it neared the island. There were also baseball box scores of games between the Washington Senators, the St. Louis Browns, and the Brooklyn Dodgers, among others.

Lorraine assumed that Rusty's interest had been the account of the U-boat plundering food from an island fisherman, so she moved on to the May editions, where the banner headline *NAVY BATTLES U-BOAT HERE* covered much of the front page of the paper on the eighth of May, along with the sub-headline *Two Blimps From Lakehurst Close In For The Kill.*

One small blurb stated that the war in Europe was over.

Then the May 17 issue declared that a German sailor had been discovered on Cooneymus Road the night before the battle to sink the U-853. It said—

Herr Gunter Schmidt is assumed to be a saboteur who had been sighted coming ashore near Dorie's Cove. He was apparently walking to the town of New Shoreham when he was tracked down and confronted by Coast Guard Seaman Second Class Cole Lonsdale from Pawtucket RI, who is credited with killing the Nazi when he attacked the mounted beach patrol with a large knife.

"There it is," Lorraine said, almost under her breath. "Cole Lonsdale from Pawtucket, Rhode Island."

The Nazi's body, the article also reported, had been taken to the Newport Navy Base for examination and burial.

"Leif, thanks for letting me poke around in your archives," Lorraine said after she placed the microfiche plates back in their protective folders and deposited them on Rusty's desk. "I think I see where Rusty was going with his article. I should be able to polish it up for Betsy so she can submit it to *Smithsonian Magazine.*"

"That's good," Leif said. "And while you're here maybe I can ask you for a big favor, since Rusty wrote perfect obituaries for islanders when they passed—and I'm not up to writing his."

Bad Santa

Lorraine drove to the south side of the island and turned off Cooneymus Road at the concrete obelisk that marked the narrow gap in the privets that was the dirt road to the Montgomery house.

"Hello, Lorraine," Dalton said when he met her at the front door. "Any news about the search?"

"Nothing good," Lorraine said. She could see that the children were sitting at the dining table with their books open. "Actually, I came to ask you for help with something that was just dropped in my lap."

"No worries," Dalton said, as he stepped outside and closed the door behind himself. "We're homeschooling so we try to have set times for the children to do their work without distractions. Now, what can I do for you?"

"Leif Carlson asked me to write Rusty's obituary."

"I see," Dalton said. "That sounds final."

"I'm afraid it is—apparently Rusty was not wearing a wetsuit when he went into the water."

"I know," Dalton said. "We ran into Hattie at the island grocery this morning and got an earful. Let's go around back so we can sit on the patio."

"I can only imagine what Hattie was saying," Lorraine said as they walked around the house to the water side, overlooking the bluffs.

"I'm sad to say that she's gossiping about the possibility that Rusty took his own life," Dalton said. "Which sounds like nonsense to me."

"I agree," Lorraine said. "Something is not right with this whole affair."

"No," Dalton said, looking down and rubbing the day-old whiskers on his chin. "Something is very wrong."

Dalton's wife came outside long enough to say hello to Lorraine and to offer them coffee or juice—Emily was a fine-looking woman in a simple dress with no makeup and a quick smile—and Dalton and Lorraine both opted for water.

"Anyway," Lorraine said after Emily left them. "Do you have some thoughts for Rusty's obit?"

"He was very genuine," Dalton said. "But one thing that I really admired about Rusty was the way he treated all people equally, whether he was talking to a fisherman or a bigwig tycoon or politician—he was always the same."

"That's a good observation," Lorraine said.

"Another thing," Dalton said. "He and Betsy have always had the most interesting friends. We went over to their house for dinner one night when an Englishman named Robin Knox-Johnson was staying with them. Do you know who that is? He was the first person ever to sail solo around the world nonstop—all the way around by himself without pulling into a single port—no one can ever do that again and be the first."

"I can hardly fathom the grit it took to complete a voyage like that," Lorraine said.

"That was Rusty's world," Dalton said. "Whether some fisherman caught a record striper or a surfer rode a fantastic wave or some local boat weathered a terrible storm at sea, Rusty was in the thick of it with a keen appreciation for those people."

"That's very insightful," Lorraine said. "I won't quote you, of course, but you've certainly given me some good ideas."

"Thank you," Dalton said. "I do worry about curiosity-seekers and my family while I'm away in Georgia where we film the show—I'm going there the week after next—that's why I'm letting my beard grow since we film the morning-after scenes first."

"I completely understand," Lorraine said.

"Tell me one thing," Dalton said. "Do you sense any foul play in this?"

"Quite frankly I'm starting to see red flags," Lorraine said. "It's hard to believe that anybody would have severe animus toward Rusty, but time will tell."

"That changes one thing for us," Dalton said. "It was so silly that I didn't think to mention it to Rossi, but Mia—my youngest—said something strange Saturday morning."

"What was that?"

"Mia is our little early bird. She is usually up before anyone else in our home, but she often stays in her room until the rest of us start moving around."

"What did Mia say?"

"She said that she saw Bad Santa walking along the bluffs behind our house just at first light. We didn't tell Rossi because it might have been something she dreamed and didn't seem important."

"Bad Santa? The movie character?"

"Yes, as played by Billy Bob Thornton with bad teeth and gnarly features—especially a big dirty beard. I think that Mia might have seen J.D. Dodge walking along the bluffs behind our house at dawn on Saturday."

Mal de Mar

Lorraine drove straight to the island airport from Dalton's house and arrived just as Connor was turning the Widgeon off the runway and taxiing to the parking area.

"How was the flight out?" she said when the engines clattered to a stop and he stepped down from the airplane to give her a hug.

"The flight was fine," he said. "But the hop home with you will be better."

"Oh?" Lorraine said as they walked to the Woody. "So, absence really does make the heart grow fonder?"

"I just don't like you being on the island without me," Connor said. "Not if some funny business is going on. Besides, your father is pestering the hell out of me with questions about Rusty that I can't answer."

"I'm not sure I'll have answers for him either," Lorraine said as they got into the Woody. "This thing is like peeling an onion—there's always another layer."

As she drove, Lorraine told him all she knew about the Nazi sailor who was shot on the island the night before the U-853 was sunk, and when they arrived at the Drake house, Connor said, "In that case we have to find out what became of Cole Lonsdale after the war. Like most veterans of that era, he probably went back to Pawtucket and lived an ordinary life."

"He might even still be alive," Lorraine said. "If I could interview him—"

"That's a long shot," Connor said. "The ranks of the Greatest Generation are getting thinner every day."

They walked into the Drake house a little before noon and found Betsy folding and stacking laundry.

"Part of Russell's simple approach to life was that he didn't have a lot of clothing," Betsy said as she folded a tee-shirt and put it on the pile. "As far as I can tell, the only things missing are his sweatshirt from the island surf shop and a pair of dungarees."

"You mean a sweatshirt like the one he gave to Ben?" Connor said. "A hoodie with a cresting-wave logo?"

"That's the one," Betsy said. "Also, I can't find his shoes. I don't suppose the searchers found them near the Woody?"

"We'll have to ask Rossi," Lorraine said. "I'll do that, because I have to talk to him before I leave the island anyway."

"Thank you," Betsy said. "Thanks for everything, both of you. You've been great."

"Don't mention it," Lorraine said. "Is your sister still coming on the noon ferry from Point Judith?"

"Yes, I want to meet her at the landing myself because I certainly don't want to risk Hattie giving her a ride—and an earful."

"In that case we better get moving," Connor said. "I flew right over the Point Judith boat when I came in to land. It was steaming past North Reef just a few minutes ago."

"Good Lord," Betsy said. "Is it almost noon? I've been so busy I lost track of time."

Connor and Lorraine got into the Woody and Betsy drove them into New Shoreham just as the *Metacomet* was arriving. Beth walked off the boat before any cars disembarked—she was shorter than Betsy, with darker hair—and she gave Betsy a big hug before hopping into the passenger seat of the Woody.

"Are you two coming back to the house?" Betsy said to Lorraine and Connor.

"Not right away," Connor said. "Look at who's coming into the harbor—that's Tony's boat, the *Racketeer*. We'll go over and say hello. Maybe Rossi can give us a ride to your house later."

"I can always come back for you," Betsy said, as she got into the Woody. "Either way, see you later."

Tony was already easing the *Racketeer* up against the pilings when Connor and Lorraine walked to the dock in front of Ballard's, where the black Humvee was waiting with the engine idling.

"That's the one called Dirk," Connor said of the Humvee driver. "He must have stayed behind on dry land today while his men were diving on the wreck."

When one of the divers jumped onto the dock to cleat the lines, Connor said, "How was it out there?"

"We need a better boat," the young man said. It was the same diver who had called the group professionals when they crossed paths at the airport, except that his fancy expedition clothing was now torn and spattered with grime.

When the other young adventurer stepped off the boat, Connor noticed that he too looked pale and exhausted as they tossed four empty scuba bottles into the Humvee and drove away without saying good-bye to Tony.

"Tony, what did you do to those kids?" Connor said with a chuckle.

"I didn't do nothing," Tony said as he untangled the rat's nest of rope that the diver had made in an amateurish attempt to make the stern line fast to a cleat. "They beat the crap out of themselves by not knowing how to stand on a deck that was rolling a little bit. Could you get that bow line for me, Connor? I can't leave it looking like some farmer tied me up."

Connor untangled the clot of rope that the other diver had wrapped around the forward cleat and secured Tony's bow with two simple round turns and a locking hitch.

"What else can I help you with?" Connor said.

"Hand me that freshwater hose," Tony said.

Connor passed the garden hose down from the dock and Tony began rinsing the salt off the boat. He had to take a scrub brush to some specks of vomit clinging to the hull.

"It doesn't look that rough out there," Lorraine said.

"It was like a millpond," Tony said. "I've never seen people get so sick on such a calm day, but I think they were all hungover. And look how those bozos scratched my fiberglass with all their fancy gear."

"That's odd," Connor said. "They made a point of telling me they were professionals."

"Yeah, right," Tony said. "They don't know crap about boats, and they know even less about diving. You should see the show they put on when they were flopping around like injured fish in the water with all their timers and spare regulators and cameras and metal detectors. I put them right on top of the wreck and they couldn't even find it before they blew through all their air. What a joke."

"I hope at least their money is good," Lorraine said.

"Oh, they're paying okay," Tony said, as he collected and rinsed the dive gear they had left strewn around the aft deck with fresh water. "But it ain't the money—I would like a little respect on my own damn boat. You know what they did, besides treating me like their cabin boy? They pulled out a joint and passed it around—freaking marijuana!—on my boat. The Coast Guard don't care who brought it aboard, I'm the captain and I would take the hit if we got boarded. So I told them next time I see or smell even one seed we're heading back to the dock and the charter is over."

"That's ridiculous," Lorraine said. "I don't care for that bunch at all."

"Right," Connor said. "I figured that out the first moment I saw them."

"Well, I suppose I can put up with them for a few more days," Tony said. "I'm coming off a slow winter—I was laid up with damn clots in my legs, you know. So it is what it is—I need the money."

"Right," Connor said. "Let me know if I can help."

Lorraine walked over to the police station with Connor after they said good-bye to Tony, and when they were halfway through the town, she turned to him and said, "I almost forgot to tell you—it seems that Dalton Montgomery's daughter saw J.D. Dodge walking on the bluffs early on Saturday morning."

"That is interesting," Connor said.

They strolled along Water Street at a leisurely pace, enjoying the day, until Connor saw the black Humvee parked alongside a large Victorian building with a long porch and a lookout tower above the red shingle roof.

"Look at that," Connor said. "Dirk's crew must have moved into the National Hotel for the week."

"I see that," Lorraine said. "And I also see who came to greet them, which smells like trouble to me."

"What are you talking about?" Connor said.

"See that beat-up BMW sedan parked next to the Hummer?" Lorraine said. "That belongs to Logan Lawrence, who happens to be a creepy wannabe lawyer renting a house on the bluffs near Rodmans Hollow."

"What are you saying?" Connor said.

"I'm saying that if Logan and the U-853 are somehow connected to Rusty's disappearance, we're going to need help out here."

"Rossi knows what he's doing," Connor said. "Let him handle this."

"Rossi is a good cop but now he is way outnumbered on this island," Lorraine said. "So right after you fly me back to Newport I'm going to call Rene Garcia. I smell big trouble with this mess—maybe we stumbled onto something serious out here—and it's high time to call out the FBI."

"In that case let's get Rossi to drive us straight to the airport," Connor said. "I have to go to my real job tomorrow morning."

4

Tuesday, May 10

The Question

A light showed in a second-floor window of the Laird house in Newport at three-thirty in the morning when Connor rolled out of bed without disturbing Lorraine and put on his airline uniform. He was scheduled to fly an Anthem Airways Boeing 737 from Boston to Miami, so he took his Glock pistol and federal flight deck officer credentials down from the lockbox in their bedroom closet and went across the hall to check on Bennett.

Connor found his son sitting up in bed messaging with someone on his laptop computer. Their old German shepherd—Bennett had named her Fenway—was sleeping alongside his bed and she raised her head and flicked her tail when she recognized Connor.

"When were you planning to sleep?" Connor said. "Reveille is at zero-six-hundred on a school day."

"Gee, I guess I lost track of time," Bennett said. "When are you coming home?"

"I have an out-and-back trip to Miami," Connor said, even though Bennett never asked where he was going, since the only thing that had mattered for many years was whether his father would be home in time for a little league game or a track meet. "I'll be home tonight, if everything goes according to plan."

"Cool," Bennett said, slipping under the blanket and closing the cover of his laptop. "Good night, Dad."

Connor was almost out the door when Bennett said, "Hey, Dad, do you think they'll ever find Rusty?"

"Nobody knows," Connor said. "Get some sleep, son."

Greatest Generation

Lorraine's alarm was set for five, but she woke up a few minutes before the buzzer and went downstairs to the kitchen, where she made a pot of coffee and sat down in the breakfast nook with her notebook computer. She was still working on a nonfiction book about Alicia Vasquez—a young woman whom she and Connor had come to know very well—who had been kidnapped from Cuba as an infant. But as she looked at the words on the computer screen, her mind kept wandering back to Rusty Drake and the name of the Coast Guardsman from the article he was working on at the time of his disappearance.

She tried to get her mind back into the Vasquez book since there would be time later in the day to finish Rusty's article on the U-853. But her reporter instincts kept telling her that name written in the margin of the first draft of her friend's article might well be the final words he had ever written—*Cole Lonsdale, Pawtucket RI.*

Lorraine reluctantly closed the word processor file of her Vasquez book and got up from the table to pour her second cup of coffee before she switched her computer to the internet.

"Oh, come on," she said under her breath, after using the name and city as search terms produced page after page of real estate listings on and near Lonsdale Avenue in Pawtucket but not a word about the man. The results were no better when she tried the name with Block Island or U-853 and a host of other search terms, until she found a twenty-year-old article from the *Providence Journal-Bulletin* archives.

"Bingo," she said to herself, when the words *Nazi Invasion of Block Island Remembered* appeared on her screen, along with a photo of an elderly man holding a sheathed knife and wearing a WWII Veteran baseball cap.

The story of the fifty-year anniversary of the events on Cooneymus Road read much like the contemporary account from 1945 in the *Block Island Times*, but it also mentioned that Lonsdale had lived on Japonica Street in Pawtucket for most of his life.

"Mom, are you talking to yourself again?" Bennett said when he came downstairs dressed for school in baggy shorts and a long-sleeve shirt. The shepherd followed close on his heels.

"Good morning, Bennett."

"I heard you say 'bingo,'" the teenager said as he hugged her from behind. "Did you hit the jackpot, or what?"

"Not quite the jackpot," Lorraine said. "This story is just coming together."

"Okay, that's cool," he said, without asking which story or what it was about.

Bennett scooped a cup of dry dog food into Fenway's bowl, which she sat near and ignored until he opened the refrigerator and added a few scraps of chicken.

"You're spoiling that dog," Lorraine said.

"I know," Bennett said as he chopped a banana onto his Cheerios along with more than enough milk.

"What are you doing today?" Lorraine said.

"Well, Nattie is working for Doc Monaco, so after school I'll probably just hang out in my room."

Which Lorraine understood to mean that he would sleep for a few hours until Natalie finished her afternoon shift at the veterinary hospital. But he washed his bowl when he was finished and hugged her one more time before leaving for school, so Lorraine chose not to comment on his sleeping habits—however bizarre they might seem to an adult.

She waited until she heard Bennett's jeep pull out of the driveway before she searched the newspaper's death notices from 1995 to the present day and found several men named Lonsdale in Pawtucket, but none with the given name of Cole or a record of service in the Coast Guard.

"Aren't you done with that Vasquez book yet?" her father said when he emerged from the downstairs bedroom, which was off the kitchen and would have been the maid's quarters a hundred years earlier.

"I'm shifting gears today," Lorraine said as she got up to pour Bertram a cup of coffee. "This story about the U-853 that Rusty was working on has piqued my interest."

"Oh, that coffee does smell grand," Bertram said as she set the cup in front of him. "So, hasn't Rusty written about that submarine before?"

"Often," Lorraine said. "The U-boat is a recurring theme in his articles and books."

"Then it sounds as if he has covered the subject quite adequately," Bertram said.

"This time is different," she said. "Rusty was working on this story the day he went missing. Maybe the last thing he ever wrote was a reference to a member of the mounted beach patrol who shot a Nazi from the U-853 on Block Island, and I've found that this old Coast Guardsman was still alive and living in Pawtucket in 1995—but he must have retired to Florida or Phoenix or somewhere, because I can't find an obituary for him."

"What makes you think this gentleman has passed?" Bertram said as he rubbed his white whiskers.

"Lonsdale would have to be eighty-five years old, anyway," Lorraine said. "Even though he enlisted as a teenager."

"Bite your tongue," Bertram said. "I'm eighty-one and still going strong. So try looking in the Rhode Island Veteran's Home for this character Lonsdale. He's probably up there in Bristol telling grand lies with the rest of the old warriors."

Farm Call

Rossi usually made a round of the island first thing every morning, but he started this day by parking his jeep on the bluffs at Rodmans Hollow and scanning the beach and the water through binoculars for a good quarter of an hour. Then he drove along the south side of the island on Cooneymus Road and pulled into the rutted dirt path to the Dodge Farm.

J.D. came barreling at him on his tractor with his beard rustling like thorny briars in the breeze as soon as the lawman's feet touched the muddy ground near his barn. He only swerved at the last moment to avoid hitting the police jeep with the front bucket.

"What are you doing here?" J.D. said. "Didn't I tell you to stay off my land?"

"Mister Dodge, why don't you step down off the tractor so we can speak like reasonable men?"

"I got nothing to say to you."

"Sure," Rossi said. "You don't have to say anything. But it might be in your own interest to hear me out."

J.D. raised his fingers to his scraggly beard and turned his head slightly to study Rossi for a few seconds before he shut off the tractor and stepped down.

"Make it quick," J.D. said as he stood crooked with his arms locked across his chest. "I got work to do, not that your kind would know anything about work."

"This won't take long," Rossi said, steeled against insults by years of working in uniform on tough city streets. "I suppose you start work early on the farm?"

"You're damn right I do. These hogs ain't known to feed and water themselves."

"How about last Saturday morning, Mister Dodge? What time did you start your chores that day?"

"What are you after?" J.D. said, looking askance at Rossi. "Get to the damn point."

"Okay," Rossi said. "Did you go for a walk along the bluffs Saturday morning?"

"That's a damn lie," J.D. said calmly and without raising his voice. "Whoever said that is a damn liar."

"I only asked you if you went for a walk," Rossi said. "I didn't say you were seen on the bluffs by Rodmans Hollow Saturday morning."

"Who said that?" J.D. said. "Tell them to come here and say that to my face and see what happens."

"I didn't say anyone saw you," Rossi said.

"You better tell me who said that," J.D. said. "I know my rights! You have to tell me who is saying that. Who is accusing me?"

"Outside a courtroom there is no such right to confront a witness," Rossi said, standing close to J.D. and the tractor. "I'm just asking a simple question."

"Damn it, I ain't got time to go for no walks," J.D. said, climbing onto the seat of his tractor. "And I ain't got time to talk to no city boy about my private business, so git! I got work to do."

Rossi saw the butt of a pistol in J.D.'s back pocket when he turned around.

"Take it easy, Julian," Rossi said, calmly pricking J.D. with his own hated first name. "You haven't answered my question—did you walk along the bluffs from Rodmans Hollow before dawn on Saturday?"

"Boy, I'm telling you for the last time—get off my land!"

When J.D. reached for his back pocket it was no contest—Rossi had taken down so many perpetrators as a city cop that his moves were instinctual. He grabbed J.D.'s skinny wrist with his left hand and pulled the farmer down off the tractor in a slow-motion arc to the ground, where he landed off balance and toppled to his butt while Rossi easily twisted the weapon away with his right hand.

"Now, Julian," Rossi said, as he stood above J.D. and unloaded the pistol. "We have to come to an understanding. I've heard that you like to wave this pistol around at people and that has got to end right now."

"That's assault!" J.D. said. "You assaulted me. I'll have you fired and run off this island before sunset!"

"I don't think I'm ready to leave quite yet," Rossi said, as he scattered the ammunition from the pistol on the ground.

"Give me back that gun," J.D. said. "You can't take it. I have a permit and I have rights."

"You don't have the right to threaten anyone with a lethal weapon," Rossi said, placing the unloaded firearm on the seat of the tractor. "Now I know you're still living in the dark ages because time has been standing still out here, but I'm here to tell you—as they say—there's a new sheriff in town. If I get any more reports about you pulling this gun on anyone, I'm going to come down here and jam it down your throat with my own hands. Do we understand each other, Mister Dodge?"

The Blade

Lorraine called the Rhode Island Veterans Home from her desk at the *Newport Daily News* that morning and was informed that Cole Lonsdale was indeed a resident there. So, after lunch she drove across the Mount Hope Bridge to Bristol and found her way through the hallways to his ward.

The old man was sitting up against pillows and a middle-aged woman was sitting at his bedside when Lorraine entered.

"You're late," the woman said. "I wondered if anyone would even care on the sixtieth anniversary. Are you from the *Pro-Jo?*"

"I care," Lorraine said. "But I'm not from the *Providence Journal.* I'm Lorraine Calhoun Laird from the *Newport Daily News.*"

"Oh?" the woman said. "Some reporter from Block Island called last week and asked a bunch of questions, but the lazy bum never showed up. Anyway, I made this easy for you and wrote everything down so you wouldn't get the story all wrong the way those numbskulls from the *Pro-Jo* did last time. Here's the story exactly the way it happened."

The woman handed Lorraine six handwritten pages that began with a list of Lonsdale's progenies including eight great-grandchildren.

"And you are—?" Lorraine said.

"Well, duh," the woman said, flipping the papers in Lorraine's hands to the last page. "Of course I signed this. I'm his daughter, see?"

"Of course," Lorraine said, turning her attention to the man in bed, who was holding a sheathed knife. "And you must be Cole. Nice to meet you, sir."

"Here's the knife," he said, speaking in a reedy voice that wheezed over his vocal cords as he offered the weapon to Lorraine with two hands as if it were a holy relic. "This is the only one—the only Nazi weapon ever captured on American soil."

"May I?" Lorraine said when she accepted the knife from him. It was heavier than she had expected with a dagger-like blade and a heavy hilt bearing a swastika. Pulling the blade a short distance out of the sheath revealed the name of *Gunter Schmidt* inscribed into the steel.

"This is quite remarkable," Lorraine said.

"He tried to kill me with that blade, but I was too quick and shot him first," Lonsdale said. "Killed him dead with one shot, I did."

"That's proof right there," the daughter said. "Some other Coast Guards saw Nazi saboteurs come ashore in other places, but Papa is the only one who shot one of them before they escaped and nobody else ever got a single piece of proof. After the war the Germans admitted that Gunter Schmidt was a crewman on that submarine but they claim he never came ashore. Liars! There's the proof that he was leading the invasion."

"Invasion?" Lorraine said.

"Yes, yes," the daughter said, pointing to her written account. "It's all in there how Papa saw the Nazi come ashore at the cove and he just knew to sit back and watch for the rest of the enemy to land."

"The cove?"

"What is it?" the daughter said. "Oh yes, Dorie's Cove—that's where the invasion was going to be. But Papa followed the man halfway to town before he pounced on him. Papa foiled their plan when this Gunter guy never cut the phone lines and came back to give the all-clear."

Lonsdale himself followed his daughter's narrative with smiles and approving nods.

"That's quite a story," Lorraine said as she handed the knife back to him. "But just to be clear, you didn't actually see an invasion—only one man. Is that correct?"

Lonsdale nodded *yes*.

"And you say you saw him come ashore on the west side of the island," Lorraine said. "And that you followed him halfway to New Shoreham on Cooneymus Road?"

Again, *yes*.

"Is a photographer going to come to take the picture?" the daughter said. "Because this time I want to be in any pictures with Papa, or forget about it."

"I'll take a few pictures," Lorraine said, pulling her 35mm Leica from her briefcase. "But I doubt these will appear in the Newport paper. However, I would like to use one in an article on the U-853 that may appear in *Smithsonian Magazine*."

"Whatever," the daughter said, posing with Lonsdale and the knife. "As long as I get credit for what I wrote there."

"The editors at *Smithsonian* are assiduous fact-checkers," Lorraine said. "But I'll be sure to mention your account."

"Okay, are we done here?" the daughter said as she took the knife from her father and wrapped it in a dish towel. "We keep the knife at home because it's too valuable to leave around here. They gave it to Papa as a prize, but now the Coast Guard Museum in New London is trying to take it back. Fat chance of that!"

"I see," Lorraine said. "Do you think that the knife may be valuable?"

"Are you kidding?" the daughter said. "This knife is priceless, and who knows how much it could get at auction with all the newspaper articles and pictures to back it up."

"I'm sure you'll treasure it always," Lorraine said.

"Oh, don't you worry. I'm the youngest but I'm the only one who comes to visit Papa and the knife is in my house so that makes it mine, and I'll get top dollar for it, you better believe."

Politics

"I guess you know why I called you over here," Tom Champlin said when Rossi came to the town manager's office.

"No doubt you got a call from J.D. Dodge," Rossi said. "I'd be interested to hear what he had to say about my visit to his farm this morning."

"He had plenty to say," Tom said. "Mostly he carried on that he wanted you fired for assaulting him."

"That's out of my hands," Rossi said. "He should file a complaint with the state police if he wants to push the issue."

"Slow down," Tom said, raising his hand slightly off his desk. "I don't think that will be necessary. I'd like to have the town attorney look into this first."

"That's your right," Rossi said. "But do you really think that the town attorney can do an impartial investigation? J.D. has been on the town council for decades and he owns a big share of the power company that keeps the lights on around here. He's done so much questionable business with the town—like winning every bid for blighted properties—that there has to be some sort of shady relationship with him and your attorney."

"I'll forget you said that," Tom said. "This looks personal because J.D. Dodge was the only town councilor who voted against hiring you even though your qualifications put you head-and-shoulders above the rest."

"You're wrong if you think that's what this is about," Rossi said. "I don't have an axe to grind with J.D., but I do need him to stop accosting hikers just because the public trail along the bluffs passes near his land. And I can't have him threatening people and brandishing a handgun in my jurisdiction."

"He's been waving that damn pistol around for years," Tom said. "Nothing ever comes of it. The damn thing probably isn't even loaded."

"It was loaded when I took it from his hand," Rossi said. "With a round in the chamber and ready to fire."

"He said that he was just reaching for a handkerchief and the gun fell out of his pocket when you dragged him off the tractor."

"That's not what happened at all," Rossi said. "Most cops would have shot him when he went for the gun."

"Why didn't you?"

"I prefer to use my hands," Rossi said.

"I see," Tom said. "Would you just give the attorney a statement? Maybe if you steer clear of J.D. for a few weeks this thing will blow over."

"That's up to J.D.," Rossi said. "As long as he behaves himself I won't have any reason to deal with him."

"Good," Tom said. "Now there's one last thing, and I'm not even sure how to broach this subject, but you know how rumors spread around a little community like this so I'll just say it—there is gossip going around like wildfire that Rusty Drake and Emily Montgomery were having an affair—not that I put any credence that nonsense, but I thought you should know."

Mobsters and Lobsters

Lorraine drove up to Providence in the afternoon and passed through the iron arch that soared across Atwells Avenue to demarcate Federal Hill from the rest of the city. She sat down in her favorite *trattoria*—an informal neighborhood place that most tourists would pass by—with her back to the brick wall.

"Nice to see you, Lorraine," Dante Colasanto said when he came out of the kitchen and sat down at the adjoining table. He was a large man in his seventies in a blue silk shirt with an open collar that exposed a heavy gold chain. "You wouldn't be here for just a cappuccino?"

"Nice to have a little pick-me-up in the afternoon," Lorraine said. "That's all."

"Come on, what gives?" Colasanto said. "Where's that fly-boy husband of yours? You never come here without him unless you want to talk about something."

"Connor is on a trip for the airline but I do have something on my mind," Lorraine said. "Tell me about Tony Marino."

"Captain Tony?" he said. "Jeez, I haven't seen Tony in what—ten years? He won't even come in here for a bowl of pasta anymore."

"But you did know him, right?"

"Sure, we was just kids when we started hanging around the stables at Narragansett. He was a real good trainer, too—until the track closed. Damn shame—he was a real good man with the ponies."

"Wasn't he also a boxer?" Lorraine said.

"Yeah, he didn't mind getting into the ring. Only he didn't trip over his laces and go down one time when he was supposed to and some friends of mine lost a lot of money. After that he started running the boat out of Newport and we didn't see him so much."

"But you kept in touch, didn't you?"

"Sure, we talked now and then. Where are you going with this, Lorraine? Tell me what I should tell you."

"My husband is friends with Tony," Lorraine said. "I just like to know what sort of people Connor is associating with."

"Tony is okay," Colasanto said with a shrug. "I got no beef with Tony."

"Yes," Lorraine said. "But isn't it true that he used to do favors for you and your associates?"

"He would tune up a player if they fell behind in their gaming debts," Colasanto said. "That's just business, you know. But he never jacked up a shop owner who didn't want to play along with the racket or anything like that. Tony was always just a nice guy with quick hands."

"How about drugs?"

"Whoa," Colasanto said. "We don't use that word in here."

"Sorry," Lorraine said. "I meant product."

"Yeah," Colasanto said. "Tony used to help some guys I knew move some things a long time ago, when they used to unload bales at the fisherman's co-op in Galilee in broad daylight. But he didn't want any part of the hard stuff and the gang-bangers—no way—so he got out of the game."

"That's interesting," Lorraine said. "But you know—I've always heard rumors that some boatman in Newport helped dispose of some—how should I say it?—unfortunate souls who came to untimely ends. Was that Tony?"

"Really, Lorraine, why would you even ask me that? Have I offended you in some way?"

"I'm the one who is sorry," Lorraine said, knowing the cue that she had stepped out of bounds. "I apologize—but I had to ask."

"That's all right," Colasanto said. "That's fine, thank you. We're friends, right? So just never go there."

"You've been very helpful, Dante," Lorraine said as she prepared to leave the table. "Thank you."

"Hey, hey," he said. "Where are you going in such a rush—have another cappuccino."

"I should really be going," Lorraine said.

"No, no, no," Colasanto said, waving the waitress in with another cup for his guest. "Your money is no good here, Lorraine. But maybe you could do a favor for me?"

"If I can," Lorraine said. "I'm guessing you have some interest in the article that I wrote about the massage parlor on Thames Street?"

"Exactly," Colasanto said.

"But that isn't your business," Lorraine said. "Those are all Asians from New York."

"That's the point," Colasanto said. "We got a good thing going in this state without the gooks coming in and messing everything up."

"Well, I did make the point that indoor prostitution has been legal since the law changed in 1980," Lorraine said. "Nobody cared as long as it was out of sight—but now these storefront massage parlors are popping up where they shouldn't, and that has to change."

"I agree," Colasanto said. "But a girl ought to be able to work if she has some class and keeps it private."

"What can I do about it?" Lorraine said.

"You can just back off a little bit, Lorraine. There's no need to change the law again. All we got to do is get rid of the storefront dives. The health department can do that easily."

"I'm surprised, Dante," Lorraine said. "Some people believe your associates were behind the change that made prostitution legal twenty-five years ago. They say it was no accident that a loophole in the law banned streetwalkers but left the hotel trade thriving."

"That could be," Colasanto said. "But hey, we don't have the power in the statehouse anymore. Those idiots are going to make it a felony for a regular guy to visit a working girl in private, and that's not right."

"I'll think about that, Dante. That's all I can say."

"Good," he said. "One other thing, Lorraine. What is Tony Marino up to that got you all worried about his business?"

"I'm still trying to figure out what his game is," Lorraine said. "Whatever it is, you'll be able to read about it in the *Newport Daily News*."

Home Is the Captain

Connor's return flight from Miami was uneventful and it was dark by the time he landed the Anthem Airlines Boeing 737 back in Boston. When he arrived home in Newport, he saw a blue SUV parked in front of his house and faint light showing in the window of Bennett's room upstairs. Bertram's windows were dark—it was nearly midnight—and Lorraine and Rene Garcia were laughing in the kitchen over a bottle of red wine.

"Hi, Connor," Garcia said when he stood up to shake hands. He was a kick-ass-and-take-names FBI agent in jeans and a leather jacket who had been ready to arrest Connor when they first met, but over the course of a long and eventful espionage investigation—the Vasquez affair—he had become a friend instead.

"I see that Lorraine is dragging you into our problem on Block Island," Connor said.

"Rene is easy," Lorraine said. "All it takes is a glass of wine and a hint of mystery to get him going."

"Maybe," Garcia said. "I'm not sure I have any business poking my nose into a missing surfer and a bunch of yahoos diving on a Nazi submarine."

"We can't let those bums get away with desecrating the gravesite of thirty-nine German sailors," Connor said. "Our friend Rusty was passionate about protecting that wreck—and his surfing accident was no accident at all. So—?"

"I'm interested," Garcia said. "I did a little research when Lorraine called me and I learned that the U-853 has been declared a National Marine Sanctuary, which was supposed to stop the taking of souvenirs. The Germans got really upset when some human remains were removed from the site in 1960."

"Sailors all over the world were pissed off by that," Connor said.

"I get it," Garcia said. "But years after those skulls and bones turned up in a private collection, legislation declaring the wreck of the U-853 a National Historic Site—which would give it total protection from souvenir hunting—has been stalled in Congress, and it doesn't appear to be going anywhere."

"That's not surprising," Lorraine said. "Washington can't get anything done these days."

"Here's the deal," Connor said. "Those guys are up to no good—I saw them at the airport loading equipment into a Humvee that could tear the wreck apart, bit by bit. I don't know what they're looking for—but if you don't stop them I will."

"Lorraine says that you know the captain of their boat," Garcia said.

"Everybody in Newport knows Tony Marino," Connor said. "He's a local character and a fixture on the waterfront."

"It's easy to see why Connor likes Tony," Lorraine said. "He's a boxer and a boatman, which just happens to be two of my husband's favorite kinds of men. But I was up on Federal Hill today and someone told me that Tony has a checkered past dating back to when he was a trainer at Narragansett Race Track."

"I wish you wouldn't go into some of those places in Federal Hill without me," Connor said.

"My sources on Federal Hill won't come near our table when you're with me," Lorraine said. "You're from different worlds and you wouldn't understand each other at all."

"Right," Connor said. "But I do understand Tony and I'm telling you that he's okay. He believes they are just doing an historical study of the U-853 and he only took the job because he can't say no to a weeklong charter this time of year—it could make or break his season."

"Okay," Garcia said. "I suppose I could go out to the island and take a look, but finding your friend Rusty is a matter for the locals, unless we come up with something that directly connects his disappearance to the crew diving on the submarine."

"When would you like to go?" Lorraine said.

"I guess I could take the ferry over tomorrow morning," Garcia said.

"Don't be silly," Lorraine said. "Connor can fly us there."

"Sure," Connor said. "I think you'll be all in after you see what's going on out there. But not too early—I've got to do a little work on the Widgeon before we launch."

Upstairs

Lorraine cleaned up the kitchen after Garcia left them while Connor went upstairs and opened the door to Bennett's room.

"Lights out, Ben," he said.

"Okay, Dad. I was just waiting for you to get home."

"Right," Connor said. "Try sleeping at night for a change, why don't you?"

"I will," Bennett said. "Sometimes I just get restless at night and can't sleep."

"Why is that, Ben? What are you thinking about when you should be sleeping?"

"I don't know," Bennett said with a shrug. "I guess I think about things like why is Mister Garcia here—is he going to help us find Rusty?"

"He's going to help me and your mother, Ben. You're going to school tomorrow."

"Sure," Bennett said. "I miss out on everything. Good night, Dad."

Then Connor went across to hall to their bedroom, and when Lorraine came up a few minutes later she said, "It's good to see Rene again. It will be great to have him on the island with us."

"I'd like it a lot more if he got back together with his wife, or moved on to the next one," Connor said.

"What?" Lorraine said. "You're jealous because I was sipping wine with him?"

"I'd like to drink some wine with you if I could," Connor said. "But we all know that would lead back to the bad times."

"Listen, fly-boy," Lorraine said, putting her arms around his shoulders. "All I'm thinking about with Rene is which one of my single friends I can hook him up with. That would be fun to watch, that's all.

"Besides," she said, dropping her arms down to his waist and looking squarely into his eyes. "You're the one who strayed over the guardrails with Ali Vasquez."

"For the umpteenth time," Connor said, "nothing happened between me and Vasquez. We're just two pilots who work together."

"Okay," she said. "I can believe that Vasquez was a fairly harmless flirtation. But are you ready to talk about that vamp Leona yet? What really happened that night of the volcano?"

"I don't want to utter that name ever again," Connor said, pushing Lorraine down on their bed. "I've got everything I'll ever need right here."

5

Wednesday, May 11

Island Games

Lorraine was standing near the Widgeon watching Connor perform his preflight inspection of the airplane when Garcia arrived at Newport State Airport. The lawman was wearing a black sweater over Levi's jeans and carrying a backpack, and Connor knew he always had a compact Glock pistol stuck into one of his cowboy boots.

"Come up and sit in the right seat," Connor said to Garcia when they went aboard. "I'll let you take the controls for a few minutes when we get up to cruising altitude."

"Thanks, Connor," Garcia said, deftly maneuvering himself into the copilot's seat next to Connor, as if he'd done it many times before. "I'll come up and enjoy the view, but I've never wanted to fly a plank."

"What?"

"You could flub around in the air on a sheet of plywood if you put a propeller on it," Garcia said. "Couldn't you?"

"You're right," Connor said, almost smiling.

"I flew Apache helicopters in the Army," Garcia said as he fastened his seatbelt. "Anything that won't launch straight up and fly sideways and backwards isn't much of a flying machine to me."

"You never told me you were a pilot," Connor said.

"You never asked."

Connor pumped the primers and adjusted the throttle and fuel mixture and propeller control levers to start the engines, and soon the satisfying vibration of the two Lycoming engines pulsed through the airframe.

"Are you all set back there?" Connor said to Lorraine after he taxied out to the runway.

"I am," Lorraine said, giving Connor a thumbs-up.

"Okay, here we go," Connor said when he lined the big twin engine airplane up on the runway centerline and pushed the throttle levers forward. The tail wheel came up almost as soon as they started to roll, and the Widgeon ambled down the runway standing tall on the main landing gears with the tail high, gathering speed until Connor coaxed the wings into the air.

"You can take the controls," Connor said after they climbed up to two thousand feet over Rhode Island Sound. "Let's head slightly east of the island since the U-853 is only nine miles away from Old Harbor— we should be able to see Tony's boat if they're out there today."

"This is like flying a truck," Garcia said once he had the yoke in his hands. "And the layout of these instruments doesn't make any sense."

"Had enough?" Connor said.

"No, this is fun," Garcia said. "I feel like we stole this contraption out of the Smithsonian and took it for a joyride."

Then Lorraine said, "I think I see Tony's boat over there."

"Yup, that's the *Racketeer*," Connor said. "It looks like Tony anchored directly over the U-853."

"How deep is the water there?" Garcia said.

"A little over one hundred feet," Connor said. "About the deepest an experienced diver feels comfortable—although the currents can be tricky."

"Have you ever dived on that wreck?" Garcia said.

"Only once," Connor said. "A few years ago I went down with some Navy buddies to take a look, but I felt like I was intruding on something that should be left alone, so I didn't stay long, never went back."

"Can we fly lower so I can take a picture?" Lorraine said.

"Let's not show our hand too soon," Connor said. "This airplane has a distinctive look and sound, and they saw me getting aboard it after I warned them not to disturb that wreck."

"Now you're thinking like a cop," Garcia said.

Connor took the controls from Garcia when it was time to descend and circled south of the island so that Lorraine could take pictures of the bluffs with her Leica camera and then he pulled the throttles back to glide the Widgeon down to the runway and touched smoothly down, one wheel at a time.

"Show-off," Garcia said when they turned off the runway.

"Don't worry," Connor said. "You'll see the Widgeon humble me next time. It's hard to make two decent landings in a row with her."

Rossi drove onto the ramp to pick them up just as Garcia was standing alongside the airplane and taking his .45 auto out of his backpack.

"I see you don't like to lose," Rossi said when he saw Garcia with the big automatic.

"You know what the old-timers say," Garcia said as he pushed the holstered weapon into his belt. "There's no second place winner in a gunfight. I'm Rene Garcia."

"Brian Rossi," the island cop said as they shook hands. "Sorry if I sounded confused when you called me last night—I was wondering why the FBI was coming out here—until you said that Connor and Lorraine were dragging you into this case."

"They're like a full-time job for me lately," Garcia said. "They can find trouble like a hound can find ticks."

"So I hear," Rossi said as they all climbed into his police jeep. "Maybe you can come look at a few things with me after I drop Connor and Lorraine at Betsy's house."

"I'd like to go with you guys too," Connor said.

"All right," Rossi said. "It shouldn't be a problem, if you hang back and let us do the heavy lifting."

Then Rossi and Garcia played the "name game" by mentioning a few law enforcement friends in Providence, where they had both worked at different times. By the time they arrived at Betsy's house each man had a good understanding of where the other was coming from by whom they liked and whom they didn't care to ride with.

"Listen to me, Lorraine," Rossi said, moments before they arrived at Betsy's house. "I have to tell you something unpleasant so I'll just say it straight—there's a nasty rumor circulating around the island that Rusty and Emily Montgomery were having an affair."

"Dalton's wife?" Lorraine said. "That's impossible."

"I know that," Rossi said. "But Betsy and Dalton both leave the island to work and leave Rusty and Emily behind. In fact, Rusty was sometimes seen with Emily when their spouses were away—and that's all it takes to start tongues wagging on a little island."

"Dear god," Lorraine said. "Please tell me that Betsy hasn't heard any of that nonsense."

"I don't think she has," Rossi said. "I'm only telling you so you can cut some fool short before they say something around Betsy that they shouldn't."

Rodmans Hollow

Rossi drove Connor and Garcia to the small clearing atop the bluffs on the south side of the island where Rusty's Woody had been found, and the men dismounted to take a look at the area. A fresh salt breeze was blowing in from the ocean.

"I wouldn't stand too close to the edge," Rossi said when Garcia looked out to the water. "These bluffs are eroding all the time."

"Right," Garcia said. "Getting down to the water looks hard enough, but it must be a tough climb to get back up here carrying a surfboard."

"Rusty knew the safe trail to the beach better than anyone," Connor said.

"How far does this other path along the top of the bluffs go?" Garcia said.

"That way is Southeast Lighthouse," Rossi said, pointing left and east. "And the other way it goes halfway around the island to the west."

"We saw some houses along the bluffs when we flew in," Garcia said. "Let's take a walk."

"Sure," Rossi said as the three men started along the trail at the top of the bluffs. "But you better check for ticks afterward. They're thick down here."

The path led along the seaward edge of a large nature preserve of low brush and small trees that had been gnarled and bent by the persistent sea breezes. A few stone walls perpendicular to the coast had once divided the acreage into pastures and planting fields, and in some places the men had to step over stones where the walls had crumbled and fallen down the bluffs into the sea.

"Wait a minute," Rossi said when they came to one pile of stones atop a cliff. "Somebody has been driving down here."

"Aren't motorized vehicles prohibited in the preserve?" Connor said.

"For sure," Rossi said. "But these look like tractor tracks, and lots of them."

"You're right," Garcia said. "It looks like they've driven right up to the edge of the bluffs, too."

"Not only that," Connor said. "Someone has been digging all around this old stone wall."

"Right," Rossi said. "It looks like somebody has been doing some illegal dumping here. There might be oil or chemicals or god-knows-what under these stones."

"We could follow the tracks," Connor said.

"No doubt they go up to Cooneymus Road," Rossi said. "They would probably disappear on the pavement. But that's okay—I know who owns this mischief—and his name is J.D. Dodge. His farm is a little farther along the bluffs."

"Who else lives down here?" Garcia said.

"There are two houses between Rodmans Hollow and the Dodge Farm," Rossi said. "Some Boston lawyer is renting one and the other belongs to Dalton Montgomery."

"Wasn't Dalton's wife the woman some people thought was having an affair with Rusty?" Garcia said. "Emily Montgomery?"

"Right," Connor said. "But that rumor that Rusty and Emily had something going on is total bullshit."

"You're probably right about that," Rossi said. "But you never know."

"Does anyone else have a motive for harming Rusty?" Garcia said.

"Actually, that would be J.D. again," Rossi said, waving toward the ocean. "J.D. is a dope, but he inherited most of the shares in the island's electric power company by being the last son of Cyrus Dodge left standing, so he is adamantly opposed to the new power-generating wind turbines they are going to build offshore, right here."

"That's right," Connor said. "And Rusty took a strong stand in favor of the wind farm in the newspaper."

"I wonder if Rusty caught J.D. doing some illegal dumping here," Garcia said. "That might have brought the issue of the environment to a head."

"Could be," Rossi said. "J.D. takes most of the waste from the power plant to some dump on the mainland that can handle hazardous materials. But there was a lot of anger about the wind farm from some people, and J.D. even stood up at a town council meeting and threatened to blow them up if they ever got built."

"Is that on the record?" Garcia said.

"Yes, but nobody takes J.D. very seriously."

"That okay," Garcia said with a sudden smile. "That's a terroristic threat—and it gives the FBI a good reason to go talk to J.D. Dodge."

"That sounds like a plan," Rossi said as they walked back to his police jeep. "But there is something else you need to know—Lorraine told me that Dalton's young daughter may have seen someone fitting J.D.'s description walking along the bluffs the morning that Rusty went missing."

"Now we're getting somewhere," Garcia said.

"Maybe," Rossi said as he stepped over the scattered stones of the ancient farm wall on the edge of the bluffs. "You never know."

Laura Ingalls

"I want to go back to work," Betsy said, sitting at her kitchen table with a cup of coffee. "I should be doing a magazine shoot in Boston today, but I don't dare leave the island. I feel like I should be here in case—"

"You can take your time," Lorraine said. "You're a great photographer and your talents will always be in demand."

"Yes, but I'm torn," Betsy said. "This is our home, but I'm not sure I want to live here without Russell."

"Come to Morristown with me and Ed," Betsy's sister Beth said. "You'd love it there, and there are so many opportunities for a photographer with your abilities."

"That's a good idea," Lorraine said. "And if you just want to get off the island for a time, you're always welcome to stay with me and Connor in Newport. You can come and go as you wish. After all, we'll be empty nesters soon and we'd love the company."

"Thank you both," Betsy said. "I like those ideas—we'll see."

"Good," Lorraine said. "For now, I'd like to finish the new story about the U-boat that Russell was working on. I think that he had unearthed some evidence about the Nazi crewman who came ashore the night before the submarine was sunk, so he might have been close to revising history by solving that mystery."

"That would be great," Betsy said.

Lorraine decided that this was not the right time to tell Betsy that she had finished Rusty's obituary, so while the two sisters talked in the kitchen, she took her coffee cup to his writing table to work on the unfinished U-boat article. He had printed a rough draft under the title *The Tightrope Walker* with numerous pen and ink corrections and questions in the margin—who was Gunter Schmidt and why had he come ashore on Block Island?

When she saw Cole Lonsdale's name written in the margin, Lorraine felt satisfied that she had followed that lead to a reasonable conclusion. So Rusty's only unexplained notation on the manuscript was the name written and underlined at the bottom of the last page—

Laura Ingalls

What is this about? Lorraine thought. Everyone knew Laura Ingalls as the author of the Little House on the Prairie books about nineteenth-century frontier life that had been wildly popular in the 1930s and 40s—not to mention the 1970s television series. Ingalls had lived until the mid-1950s, but what did that have to do with a Nazi U-boat?

Unless, Lorraine thought—unless Gunter Schmidt was somehow distantly related to the Ingalls family. Perhaps he had jumped ship to make contact with them to live in America after the war?

"Betsy," Lorraine said, when she got up from Rusty's writing table. "Can I borrow the Woody? I have to check on something at the *Times*."

Grandfathered Rights

"We should talk about this," Rossi said when he pulled his jeep to the side of Cooneymus Road a mile away from the Dodge Farm and turned in his seat to face Connor and Garcia. "There are a few things about J.D. Dodge you ought to know first."

"I'm listening," Garcia said.

"For starters, the last time I was here I had to grab a loaded pistol out of his hand and take him down to the ground."

"And you didn't arrest him?" Garcia said.

"There was no point in escalating a feud with a member of the town council," Rossi said. "J.D. has been waving that pistol around for years and I've received a few calls about him threatening hikers on the Bluffs Trail, but I couldn't charge him unless someone was willing to swear a complaint. That's okay—sooner or later I'll get an indictment for something big and lock him up for good."

"Good to know," Garcia said.

"Also, I didn't tell him that it was just a kid who saw him walking on the bluffs Saturday morning," Rossi said. "Dalton and Emily are the only couple near here with young children so we don't want J.D. causing trouble for them."

"Got it," Garcia said. "Who else lives on the farm?"

"Nobody," Rossi said. "J.D.'s wife was standing behind the tractor one day when he backed against a stone wall. That was long before I was on the job out here—but it was described as a horrible accident."

"I don't think I'm going to like J.D. very much," Garcia said.

"So, Connor," Rossi said, "you should probably stay in my jeep while we talk to him."

"No deal," Connor said. "I'm a sitting duck in the backseat. I'd rather stand outside where I can defend myself, if it comes to that."

"Are you carrying?" Rossi said.

"Yes, I am."

"You don't have to worry about Connor," Garcia said. "He was solid when we got into a jam in Mexico."

"Okay," Rossi said as he drove toward the farm. "I'll buy you a beer after this so you can tell me all about that one."

J.D. was nowhere in sight when they arrived at his farm, but a rusted dump truck and his green 1972 Cadillac El Dorado were parked near the house. The tractor was sitting outside the barn, so Garcia hitched his sweater up to expose his .45 and his gold badge when he got out of the vehicle and said, "Let's try the barn."

The ground between the house and the barn was muddy and criss-crossed by tractor tire tracks except for one set of narrow tracks from a small car that led into the barn. Connor stayed near the police vehicle, but when Rossi and Garcia got closer to the tractor, they noticed that the motor was idling so they were not surprised when J.D. stepped out of the big barn doors wiping his hands with a rag.

"Damn it, Rossi," J.D. said. "Didn't Tom Champlin tell you to steer clear of me?"

"I don't let the town manager run my office," Rossi said. "Besides, I'm here with the FBI today—and the Feds are notoriously trigger-happy—so keep calm and keep your hands where we can see them."

"That's right," Garcia said, flashing his credentials. "I'm Special Agent Garcia from the Providence office of the FBI, and you are on the record for making threats against the proposed offshore wind farm, Mister Dodge. We need to talk about that."

"Hold on a damn minute," J.D. said, tossing the rag to the ground. "That was just talk and we've still got freedom of speech in this country. I didn't do nothing wrong."

"Making terroristic threats against the nation's power grid is a federal offense, Mister Dodge."

"What?" J.D. said. "I ain't no Arab raghead and I didn't make no terror threat. I'm a duly elected official and I can say anything I damn well please at a town council meeting, and you better get that straight, Mister FBI."

"There's no point in arguing here," Garcia said. "I'm officially informing you that any further threats against the wind farm project will result in your arrest—it's that simple. Do you understand that, Mister Dodge?"

"Listen here," J.D. said. "My family has held this soil for two hundred years so I really don't give a damn what you say—now get off my land."

"Really?" Garcia said. "Two hundred years? There must be a lot of farm animals buried on this land."

"What do you care?" J.D. said.

"I hope not recently," Rossi said. "It's illegal to bury animals or offal in the ground anywhere in the state these days."

"What I do when I slaughter a hog is my business," J. D. said. "I got grandfather rights to do whatever on this land."

"How about in Rodmans Hollow?" Rossi said. "Is that where you dispose of the hazardous waste from the power company?"

"Hell no," J.D. said. "I take all the old transformers and whatnot off the island. I got a safe place for all that stuff where it don't bother nobody."

"The transformers are loaded with PCBs," Garcia said. "That stuff is deadly if it leaks into the groundwater."

"I know that!" J.D. said. "That's why I got paperwork to show it is all stored in a safe place until it can be disposed of, all nice and legal-like."

"That's fine, Mister Dodge," Rossi said. "We'll look into that later. Have a nice day."

Then the two lawmen turned back to Rossi's jeep, where Connor was waiting.

"What do you think?" Rossi said, after they got into his jeep.

"I think we have to dig up this place," Garcia said.

"Do you really think that J.D. killed Rusty?" Connor said. "That he might be buried out in the field somewhere?"

"He's guilty as sin," Rossi said. "I'll get a warrant and call the state police."

"Damn it," Connor said. "What do I say to Betsy?"

"Not a damn thing," Garcia said. "We didn't even talk to J.D. today."

Table With A View

"Betsy, let's get out of the house for a while," Lorraine said, when she got back from her brief visit to the newspaper office. "The men want to meet us at Ballard's for lunch."

"That would be nice," Betsy said.

Beth quickly agreed, and soon the three women were driving into the town of New Shoreham, where they found Connor, Rossi, and Garcia sitting at a table in the restaurant with a commanding view of Old Harbor.

Lorraine introduced Garcia to Betsy and Beth and after they sat down she said, "What did you boys find today?"

"Nothing certain yet," Connor said. "How about you?"

"Actually, I made an interesting little discovery in the archives of the *Block Island Times*," Lorraine said. "The first draft of Rusty's article on the U-853 ended with a cryptic notation. He had handwritten the name of Laura Ingalls on the last page."

"Ingalls the writer?" Connor said.

"Maybe," Lorraine said, "but I had to dig deep into a copy of the *Times* from 1944 to find a mention of her name. It turns out that Laura Ingalls did visit Block Island during the war because there was a little blurb in the society column amid news of the bridge club and the book club and the First Settlers Society. Here is what I found, word for word." She opened her notebook and read aloud—

"Visitor of note aviatrix Laura Ingalls of New Haven arrived on the Tuesday boat to be received at the home of Hattie Wagner, where she may remain for two weeks of vacation after paying her debt to society. Many island residents will recall that Miss Ingalls was a frequent visitor to our island in years gone by. No public engagements have been announced."

"What the hell is an aviatrix?" Rossi said.

"That's a fairly dead word," Lorraine said. "The term 'aviator' was so loaded with macho connotation in the 1930s that the newspapers of the day needed a word for female pilots, and some wag came up with 'aviatrix.'"

"That's quaint," Garcia said. "Maybe the writer got her pilot's license late in life, but that line about 'paying her debt to society' doesn't fit my impression of Laura Ingalls. Wasn't she supposed to be a symbol of America's virtuous pioneer spirit?"

"Exactly," Lorraine said. "That's why this is so confusing."

"It's not confusing at all," Connor said. "You apparently have the wrong Laura Ingalls."

"Oh?" Lorraine said. "Would you care to enlighten us, fly-boy?"

"There was some woman pilot who was also named Laura Ingalls trying to set world records in the 1930s," Connor said. "Except that she sometimes used her mother's maiden name—Houghtaling—so I think you're talking about Laura Houghtaling Ingalls."

"You never cease to amaze me," Lorraine said. "How could you possibly know that?"

"That's easy," Connor said. "I've often wished I could have been a pilot in the halcyon days of aviation, and I've read every book I could find about that era."

"So what did this Laura Ingalls do that was so special?" Rossi said. "I never heard of her."

"That's because she didn't do much," Connor said. "Except that she came from an upper-crust family in New York that had a lot of money to buy her the best new airplanes. And Lindbergh's nonstop solo flight to Paris in 1927 had fired the public's imagination, so anyone with a hot airplane was trying to do something to get into the record books. But this woman was just a publicity hound and the records she went after were mostly meaningless, so history has all but forgotten her."

"What do you mean by meaningless?" Betsy said.

"She would go aloft and fly hundreds of loops and rolls over some city. Then her publicity department would make it sound like some great aeronautical feat, and the newspapers would eat it up, even though pilots know that you can do simple maneuvers like that until the airplane runs out of fuel, if you have nothing better to do. She was also the first person to fly solo around South America in 1934, but nobody really cared or paid much attention, since Wiley Post had already flown solo around the world in 1933."

"Aren't you being a little sexist?" Lorraine said. "After all, you don't consider the records set by Wiley Post and Lindbergh to be meaningless."

"Get this straight," Connor said, "there were a few gals doing great flying in the old days. Louise Thaden, Blanche Noyes, and Jackie Cochran had the guts and skill to fly the hottest ships fast and far, and they made some real advances in aeronautics. Cochran even beat the military pilots in the transcontinental air race to win the Bendix Trophy one year. So it's just my opinion, but I wouldn't put Ingalls in that class."

"She must have done something right," Lorraine said.

"Nope," Connor said. "As far as I know she was more famous—or infamous—for her wacky political views. Ingalls was hooked up with Lindbergh when he was pounding the drum for that America First nonsense before the war, but she carried it too far, and some of her fiery speeches were spiked with Nazi salutes and anti-Semitic venom. She was a Nazi at heart, and I remember reading that she even went to prison for being too cozy with some official in the German embassy with ties to the Gestapo."

"Now I remember," Garcia said. "Ingalls was the first person prosecuted for violating FARA—the Foreign Agents Registration Act—which was passed in 1938 over concerns for a large number of Nazi sympathizers who had become naturalized American citizens."

"That's great," Lorraine said. "Now I see where Rusty was going with his article. He must have found some connection between Ingalls and the Tightrope Walker—which was the name he had given to the mystery man from the U-853."

"I like that name for the mystery man," Connor said. "And it does sound plausible that Ingalls would rendezvous with a Nazi operative. But you just quoted the *Times* as saying that Ingalls was on the island for two weeks in 1944, and the U-853 sunk in May of 1945."

"That is a problem," Lorraine said. "Clearly, I'm going to have to do more research."

"Maybe I can help you with that," Garcia said. "There has to be a file about this mystery man from an enemy U-boat, and any Nazi sympathizers on the island would have been thoroughly investigated. I'll ask a friend of mine in Washington to dig into the FBI archives to see what she can find."

When their food arrived—chowder and clam cakes and steamed littlenecks and lobster rolls and beers all around except for Connor, who got a ginger ale—their waitress offered a kind word to Betsy and allowed how she would miss Rusty's writing in the *Times*.

"Thank you," Betsy said. "That means a lot to me."

They were eating heartily when Hattie entered the restaurant and came straight to their table.

"I saw Rusty's Woody outside and I just had to come in to see you," Hattie said, hovering at their table. "Betsy, I'm so happy you're getting out and around. Everything happens for a reason, you know. My brother was only nine when he got killed in the fire—burned to death, the poor little boy—but I know everything happens for a reason and don't you worry, time heals all, and you just have to get on with living. 'Life is for the living,' my mother used to say."

"I'm sorry to hear about your brother," Betsy said, forcing a smile. "But I'm fine, thank you. Please have a good day."

Betsy seemed to have lost her appetite and only picked at her food after Hattie left them, so before long Beth said, "We should probably be getting back to the house."

"I'll get a ride with Rossi," Lorraine said, deciding to stay with the men when Betsy and Beth drove home in the Woody. They had just finished devouring the seafood on the table when the *Racketeer* slipped into the harbor and tied up to the dock in front of Ballard's. The divers jumped off Tony's boat as soon as it was against the pilings and got into the Hummer to drive the short distance to the National Hotel.

"I'd like to know who those guys really are," Connor said, "because they don't know squat about boats or diving."

"I could just demand to see some identification," Rossi said, "but then they would know we were on to them."

"Right," Garcia said. "We might be better off just watching them until they make their move—whatever it might be."

"Oh, by the way, Connor," Lorraine said as they watched Tony wash the decks of his boat with a freshwater hose from the pier. "While I was up on Federal Hill yesterday I happened to see Dante Colasanto."

"I wish you wouldn't mention Tony to that old mobster," Connor said.

"I had to," Lorraine said. "I needed to gauge his reaction."

"Really?" Garcia said. "Colasanto has the perfect poker face. He wouldn't say crap, even if he had a mouthful of it."

"Not to you," Lorraine said, "but I think that Dante has some real affection for Tony. I got the impression that they let him out of their gang before he got in too deep, simply because he wasn't cut out for the rackets."

"That would be a first," Rossi said. "The mob doesn't cut anyone loose just because they're a nice guy."

"In this case," Lorraine said, "I think they did."

"I agree," Connor said. "I've known Tony for years and I think the world of him. Anyone on the waterfront will tell you he's a good man with a big heart."

"It's amazing he goes boating with those legs," Lorraine said, when Tony finished securing the *Racketeer* and waddled across the dock toward the restaurant with a shuffling gait. "It looks like he's in real pain when he moves."

"The boat isn't sport for Tony," Connor said. "It's his livelihood. He's one of those old guys who doesn't know how to quit working."

"Much like an old airline pilot I know," Lorraine said, tilting her head toward Connor as if sharing a secret with Garcia and Rossi.

After being on the water all morning, it took Tony's eyes a few seconds to adjust to the softer indoor light when he entered the restaurant, but he smiled when Connor said, "Hello, Captain, come over and join us."

"Thanks," Tony said as he sat. "Any news about your friend Rusty?"

"Nothing," Connor said. "How's your charter going?"

"Awful. I think I'm all done. These bozos are so clueless they're going to hurt themselves."

"Tell us about it," Lorraine said. "What are they doing on the submarine?"

"Underwater archaeology—supposedly," Tony said. The waitress put a beer in front of him and he began drinking from the bottle as he spoke. "But they don't know crap about the ocean. Like when Rusty is still missing off the island so I tell them to keep a lookout at all times, but they just sit around talking in a circle all day. And you ought to see them putting on their dive gear like a bunch of first-timers who don't know nothing. By the way, who are your friends?"

"Brian Rossi is the new island cop," Connor said, "and this is our friend Rene Garcia."

"Nice to meet you guys," Tony said. "But why are two cops watching my boat anyhow?"

"Connor didn't say I was a cop," Garcia said.

"No, he didn't," Tony said, "but I could make you as a Fed with my eyes shut."

"Right, I'm FBI," Garcia said, showing his identification. "And I'm not surprised that the skipper of a boat named *Racketeer* has a sharp eye for law enforcement,"

"Listen, the boat's name is just an inside joke," Tony said. "Yeah, I got a little mixed up with some shady characters when I was younger, but I avoid those guys now. Go ahead and search my boat from stem to stern if it will make you feel any better. Like I said, I'm all done with this charter and I just hope their checks clear the bank because there's something fishy about this whole deal."

"I wouldn't want you to cancel your charter at this point," Garcia said. "We don't know whether your customers are engaged in any criminal wrongdoing. I'd rather you stick with it until we know what they're up to."

"Look, I know how you government men work," Tony said. "If those guys are breaking the law, I'm an accessory or whatever, and you'll seize my boat and take the money they paid me as evidence—and then I'll have nothing."

"Just be straight with me and that won't happen," Garcia said. "I guarantee you'll be protected."

"No," Tony said. "You might have noticed that I'm too old to start all over again, so please just let me walk away from this deal."

"Tony, I wouldn't worry about that," Lorraine said. "Special Agent Garcia just made that offer in front of the island chief of police and a newspaper reporter. So you're covered."

"Really?" Tony said.

"Really," Garcia said. "Just be truthful with me and you'll come out ahead of the game."

"Okay," Tony said, as he got up to leave them. "I'm living on the boat while I'm out here, so you know where to find me, and I'll just keep doing what I do."

"There is one thing," Garcia said after Tony was standing. "I'll need the names of your divers, and their dates of birth and addresses if you have them."

"I'll give you everything I have," Tony said. "I had them each write their name and address in my logbook the first day."

"That's good," Rossi said. "I'll stop by the *Racketeer* when we leave here and copy that information."

Late Arrival

"Well, look at this," Lorraine said, looking out the window after Tony left them. A muddy BMW sedan drove past the pier where the *Racketeer* was tied up and then parked in front of the National Hotel. "That's Honey, Logan's girlfriend."

"It sure is," Rossi said. "And she's going into the hotel where the divers are staying."

"That's interesting," Connor said.

"It's more than interesting," Garcia said. "Honey's BMW has New York license plates, and so does the Hummer that the divers are driving around the island." He turned to Rossi and said, "Have you run those plate numbers yet?"

"Yes," Rossi said. "I checked the BMW's plate the day after Rusty's Land Rover was found not far from the house Logan is renting, and it came back to a corporation in Manhattan."

"Does Logan work for that company?" Lorraine said. "Because he told me he's an attorney in Boston with an office in the Millennium Tower—but he's not listed in the directory for that building. In fact, I can't find anyone who ever heard of a lawyer by that name anywhere in Boston."

"I don't know about that," Rossi said. "His name wasn't on the registration, but the car didn't come back as stolen or wanted for any offense, so…"

"How about the Hummer?" Garcia said.

"The Hummer is registered to Dirk Novak in East Hampton."

"That's the lead diver," Connor said. "I heard one of the other men call him Dirk when I first saw them unloading their gear at the airport."

"Okay," Garcia said, "we'll have to start investigating all of these names and start a case file."

"I'll get on the computer as soon as I get back to my office," Rossi said.

"Wait a minute," Lorraine said, "are you saying that these New Yorkers are connected to Rusty's disappearance?"

"I'm saying that I'm going to stay on the island tonight," Garcia said. "I noticed that the National Hotel has their vacancy sign out—I think I'll walk over and check in."

"But won't the divers make you as a cop?" Lorraine said.

"You'd be surprised how quickly I can get interested in real estate," Garcia said. "That's one of my favorite covers."

"But you identified yourself as FBI to J.D.," Connor said.

"That's okay," Garcia said. "If J.D. is also talking to the divers, that tells us something important, too."

"Yes," Lorraine said, "but if you spook the divers and they clear out, how will we know what they've been doing on the U-boat?"

"The way I see it," Connor said, "sooner or later we're going to have to go down to the U-853 and see for ourselves."

"Exactly," Garcia said.

"I could have the state police dive team out here in a few hours," Rossi said.

"It will probably come to that in the end," Garcia said. "But that would be a big operation that the bad guys couldn't miss. Maybe we can pull off a surreptitious dive down to the wreck and take a look around without them even knowing we were there."

"You're talking a covert night dive?" Connor said. "It's deep, and there is a current to contend with."

"No guts, no glory," Garcia said.

"Since you put it that way—I'm all in," Connor said. "I'll see what Rusty has in his shed for dive gear and I'll bring my own stuff when I come back to the island."

"Connor, don't you dare," Lorraine said.

"We can talk about it on the flight back to Newport," Connor said. "But I can't let Garcia have all the fun."

"Fine," Lorraine said. "I'll stay on the island tonight, too. Because I agree—we can't let Rene have all the fun."

6

Thursday, May 12

Guilty Pleasure

Lorraine was having a light breakfast with Betsy and Beth when the sisters announced they were going to the island grocery, so she asked them to give her a ride to the National Hotel, where she found Garcia sitting in the dining room with coffee and a copy of the *Block Island Times*.

"Good morning, Rene," she said. "How was your night?"

"Quiet," he said. "The divers got in the black Hummer and went down to the *Racketeer* a half hour ago. But it's probably not going to be a fun day on the water, judging by their hang-overs from last night."

"How long did Honey stick around yesterday?"

"Not long," Garcia said. "She had a few drinks with the divers before she left in her BMW, and then the guys sat at the bar the rest of the night until they disappeared up to their rooms—except for Dirk. He took off in the Hummer at ten o'clock and didn't come back until after midnight."

"That's interesting," Lorraine said. "I wonder where Dirk went for those two hours?"

"Me too," Garcia said. "I called Rossi as soon as Dirk left this place, of course, and he looked around the island without spotting the Hummer until it showed up back here."

"What do you make of that?" Lorraine said. "Because I have a good guess."

"I know exactly what you're thinking," Garcia said. "And yes, Dirk and Honey were pretty chummy at the bar. They might have hooked up at some secluded spot where Rossi wouldn't have seen them. There's no shortage of dirt roads and trails back into the bushes on this island."

"You know, Rene," Lorraine said, "sometimes it is scary how much we think alike."

"Cops and journalists are both students of human nature," Garcia said.

"Yes, we are," Lorraine said, dropping her chin into her hand with her elbow on the table and looking directly at him. "And some people are more fun to study than others."

"I'm too transparent to be entertaining," Garcia said. "You, on the other hand, are an enchanting woman, Lorraine."

"You have no idea how it feels to be flattered by a handsome younger man," she said. "Especially a totally built man with a gun in his cowboy boot—even though we both know that nothing can ever come of it."

"I know," Garcia said. "I'm just your guilty pleasure. So, would you like to take a walk over to Rossi's office? It will be interesting to hear what he's found out."

"Sure, let's go," Lorraine said as they stood up to leave. Then, when they were almost out the door, she laughed and said, "Enchanting? Really, Rene, you are so full of crap."

College of War

"Good morning, Bertram," Connor said when the ambassador came into the kitchen of the Laird house in Newport. "Did you get a good night's sleep?"

"I always do," Bertram said. "May I join you for breakfast?"

"Of course," Connor said. Then he turned to Bennett—who was furiously scooping Cheerios and banana slices out of a bowl and into his maw—and said, "Ben, stop feeding your face long enough to say good morning to your grandfather."

"Hi, Grandpa," Bennett said as he jumped up from the table and rinsed his bowl in the sink. "Sorry, I'm late for school."

The men had a leisurely breakfast of fruit, oatmeal, and toast after the teenager left them, until Bertram said, "Connor, do you have the time to take me to the navy base this morning? I'd like to take a look at some of the artifacts from the U-853 in the War College Museum."

"Sure," Connor said. "That's a great idea. I'd like to see that stuff again myself."

They left the house in Connor's pickup truck and drove past the Viking Hotel and the Quaker houses of the Colonial seaport to Gate 1 at the Newport Navy Base. The museum was housed in a stone building atop a hill on Coasters Island, with a commanding view of the Verrazano-Pell Bridge spanning the East Passage of Narragansett Bay. In 1890 this had been the home of the Naval War College, which had long ago moved to a much larger and more modern complex nearby.

The propellers from the U-853—which had been blasted off the sunken submarine years earlier by souvenir hunters—had been placed on display alongside the flagpole in front of the museum, along with a plaque commemorating the sailors of all nations who had died in the Battle of the Atlantic.

When they went inside, Connor was surprised to see Professor Sergei Mikhailov standing near the door to greet them, and Connor said, "What the hell are you doing here, Sergei?"

The Russian was a few years younger than Bertram, with unkempt white hair, a cardigan sweater, and a Naval War College identification card hanging around his neck. As one of the world's foremost experts on human intelligence techniques—person-to-person contacts—the US Navy had been eager to recruit Mikhailov when he defected to the West.

"I asked Professor Mikhailov to join us today," Bertram said. "At my request he has been looking into your mystery man from the U-853. After all, who better to investigate a Nazi spy or saboteur than a former spy himself?"

"Except that I'm not so sure about the 'former' part," Connor said. "Once a KGB man, always a KGB man. Isn't that right, Sergei?"

"I like America now," Sergei said, with a smile. "And I appreciate the opportunity to assist you in this matter, Connor. You see, Lorraine sent me a copy of the article your friend Rusty was writing, and I believe that I have found some useful insights into this man he called the Tightrope Walker. Now that I have looked into this affair, I may use it in my lectures as an example of how not to conduct a counterespionage investigation."

Connor said, "Are you implying that the investigation was bungled?"

"Absolutely," Sergei said as they walked to the display case containing artifacts from the U-853—an officer's hat, linens, and an escape breathing apparatus—and photographs of the depth-charge attack that destroyed her. "The most egregious error was that the body of the Tightrope Walker was cremated before he was positively identified, and the ashes were unceremoniously scattered at sea."

"The Navy must have taken fingerprints and photographs of the corpse?" Bertram said.

"They certainly did," Sergei said. "However, the photographs that might have been used to identify this man after the war were last seen in the bottom drawer of the commodore's desk. It seems that the officer who led the attack on the U-853 had convinced himself that the man was Gunter Schmidt—a crewmember from the U-boat that was his personal victory—so there was no imperative to turn the full-face pictures over to Naval Intelligence."

"How can you be so sure that the commodore wasn't right?" Connor said. "After all, the Tightrope Walker was carrying Gunter Schmidt's Hitler Youth knife when he was shot."

"Because the Germans keep meticulous records," Sergei said. "So we now know that Machinist Gunter Schmidt aboard U-853 was nineteen years old with blond hair and blue eyes. And US Navy autopsy records indicate that the man you call the Tightrope Walker had brown hair and hazel eyes—and that he was approximately thirty-five years of age and one inch taller than Schmidt."

"Wouldn't those differences have been obvious once our navy had the German crew records?" Connor said.

"The logbooks and patrol reports of all 1,250 U-boats commissioned into the Kriegsmarine were turned over to the Allies immediately after the war," Sergei said, "along with crew lists for each patrol. But the Kriegsmarine retained most of the personal data for individual crewmen in their own archives for many years."

"At some point the Navy must have realized that the man who was shot on Block Island was not an ordinary crewman from the U-853," Bertram said.

"Absolutely," Sergei said. "After the war the Navy blamed the misidentification on the doctors who performed the autopsy, since they were ordinary medical doctors, not forensic pathologists."

"We know how that works," Connor said. "The brass hats didn't want to admit that the commodore screwed the pooch. But what became of the full-face pictures?"

"The commodore jealously guarded the only copies," Sergei said. "Apparently he was going to write a book, but he died shortly after the war ended and the photographs were lost."

"So let me ask you this," Connor said. "Who was the Tightrope Walker?"

"Perhaps he was a saboteur," Bertram said. "We know that the Nazis landed teams of spies and explosives on the East Coast with the intention of disrupting our war industries."

"You're speaking about Operation Pastorius," Sergei said. "That was early in the war—1942—and it was a complete failure for the Nazis, who vastly underestimated the American industrial capacity. They were foolish to believe that setting off a few explosives in factories would scare workers away from the assembly lines."

"Right," Connor said. "As long as we're speculating, let me run this by you—what if the Tightrope Walker was a Nazi official attempting to evade trial for war crimes by coming to America?"

"That's not as crazy as it sounds," Bertram said. "Germany was defeated by May of 1945—Hitler was dead and the Russians were in Berlin—and we know that some Nazi leaders followed their ratlines to Argentina and other places where they could blend with the populace. Why not America, where upwards of twenty percent of our population were recently naturalized citizens from Germany? And let's not forget that thousands of Nazi sympathizers from the German-American Bund had gone underground after we entered the war."

"Correct," Sergei said. "Similarly, he could have been a Nazi official here to negotiate the terms of Germany's surrender, much like Deputy Fuhrer Rudolph Hess parachuting into Scotland in 1941. But I have a much more intriguing theory to offer to you—I believe it is very possible that your Tightrope Walker came to American shores to continue the struggle for National Socialism."

"That is intriguing, indeed!" Bertram said. "If I understand you, the Tightrope Walker may have been on a mission to continue the Nazi agenda by political means—perhaps he meant to infuse American popular culture and politics with Ethnic Nationalist ideals?"

"Bingo," Connor said. "That would explain why he might have been attempting to connect with a Nazi-loving anti-Semite like Ingalls—to stoke the embers of ethnic hate that had long been simmering here. But that doesn't answer the main question—who was the Tightrope Walker?"

"If I may, I would like to suggest one possibility," Sergei said. "As you know, the Russian Army was in a position to make the most thorough accounting of the fates of all known Nazi officials after the war. By comparing the Red Army records with those of the Kriegsmarine, some researchers have noted that one of Joseph Goebbels's key aides disappeared in February 1945—two weeks before the U-853 departed on that final voyage to the American East Coast."

"That is too extraordinary to be a coincidence," Bertram said.

"I agree," Sergei said. "But the matter has been debated in academic circles for years, as has the fate of so many Nazi officials. There were other ratlines this aide to Goebbels might have followed out of Germany, if he is not buried under the rubble of bombed-out buildings in Berlin. However, one fact stands out for me—this young man had lived in America as a child so he was fluent in English. Moreover, he was known to speak some Hungarian."

"I think I see where this is going," Connor said. "People have forgotten that Hungary allied themselves with the Nazis and declared war on Russia in 1941, until the Wehrmacht was defeated at Stalingrad. Some of the Nazis discovered in South America after the war claimed to be displaced persons from Hungary who were simply swept up in the changing fortunes of war. Am I right?"

"Exactly," Bertram said. "Hungarian citizenship—rather than German—would have been a convenient cover story for the Tightrope Walker—if he had lived. But influencing American post-war politics would have been a tall order for one man. I would think he would have to possess considerable resources."

"To that end," Sergei said, "some historians have theorized that the Nazis had such wealth hidden in American banks and corporations, ready to be tapped after the war. Remember, Hitler hoped for the war to end in a standoff with the Allies."

"Maybe," Connor said. "Or maybe the Tightrope Walker brought his fortune along on the U-853. So, who is this man?"

Sergei said, "I believe—possibly—that your Tightrope Walker was Goebbels's most virulent young propagandist—Sebastian Klaus."

Lucky Break

Rossi was sitting behind his desk shuffling paper between his in and out baskets when Lorraine and Garcia entered his office.

"That's a lot of paperwork for one small island," Garcia said.

"Everybody seems to have a question or a complaint of some kind," Rossi said with a shrug. "And it all ends up on my desk, sooner or later. But let me tell you what I found when I ran checks on our boys." He handed a few computer printouts to Garcia and said, "Dirk Novak is apparently a trust-fund baby who hasn't worked a day since he graduated from Princeton. As far as I can tell, he's blown through most of his inheritance playing at thrill sports like parachuting and racing cars, because when I ran a credit check on him it came up with red flags for unpaid debts."

"No surprises there," Garcia said. "How about his posse?"

"Dirk's pals—he calls them Rick and Brownie—are two bottom-feeders with arrests for shoplifting, passing bad checks, and drug possession in Virginia and Florida. Not exactly model citizens, but not violent offenders, either."

"How about Honey?" Garcia said. "How does she fit into this?"

"I don't have a bead on her yet," Rossi said, "or Logan. He rented the house through a real estate company two years ago and the rent has been paid every month, so they don't particularly care that his name is an alias."

Lorraine said, "What makes you think he's using a bogus name?"

"The rental agent screwed up," Rossi said. "She never made a copy of his photo ID when she wrote the lease, and the bills are all being paid by checks from a Delaware corporation."

"That's good," Garcia said, "it gives us a reason to lean on him a little harder."

"In that case you'll really like the next part," Rossi said. "I know that he's lying about being a lawyer because nobody named Logan Lawrence is licensed to practice law in Massachusetts or New York. In fact, the only lawyers by that name live in Colorado and Florida—and they are both at least seventy years old."

"Now I know we should go have a talk with Logan," Garcia said.

"Right," Rossi said, glancing at Lorraine and then back to Garcia. "And about that other thing—the state police are ready to move whenever we give the word."

"What 'other thing' is that?" Lorraine said.

"It's probably not important," Rossi said. "You don't need to worry about it."

"That's fair," Lorraine said. "I wouldn't want to intrude on your little cop secrets, but I could use a lift back to Betsy's house if you're going that way."

"Don't worry, Lorraine," Garcia said as they walked outside and got into Rossi's jeep. "When we're ready to nail these characters, you'll be the first to know."

Rossi started the jeep and they had hardly pulled away from the police station when a muddy sedan came speeding into town from the south side of the island. The BMW—with Honey behind the wheel—rolled through the intersection and made a turn directly in front of them.

"How lucky can we get?" Rossi said, when he switched on his flashing lights and spun the wheel around to pull up behind Honey as she arrived at the ferry landing. The boat had already backed into the slip and passengers were streaming off when she finally stopped her car.

"What's wrong with you?" Honey said, jumping out of the car and accosting Rossi, who had dismounted with his summons book in hand. "I'm going to miss the ferry!"

"Get back in the car, ma'am."

"No!" Honey screeched, getting in Rossi's face. "I haven't done anything wrong."

"You just failed to come to a complete stop and signal a turn," Rossi said, leading her to the back of her car. "License, registration, and proof of insurance, please."

"It's in the damn car," Honey said. "Are you going to be a complete asshole and make me miss the ferry over a stupid turn signal?"

"Stay here," Rossi said as he opened the passenger-side door to her car and reached into the glove box. Then he brought her purse to the back of the BMW and set it on the trunk, where she could fish her wallet out.

"Make this quick," Honey said as she handed him her license. "I'm going to miss the damn ferry. This is the dumbest thing ever."

"The Rhode Island vehicle code requires a turn signal—" he looked at her license and read the name— "Miss Valentine. I'm just doing my job."

Rossi wrote the ticket and gave it to Honey, who threw him the finger as she drove onto the ferry.

"There goes Michelle Valentine, from Astoria, New York," Rossi said when he got back behind the wheel of his jeep. "Date of birth, January 5, 1981."

"Are you just going to let her leave the island?" Lorraine said.

"We don't have a valid reason to stop her," Rossi said. "But now that we know who she is, I'm betting we can find her again if we have to."

"She won't be able to hide for too long," Garcia said. "But now that we have a positive ID on her, we should go back to the police station and do some research before we talk to Logan—right after we give Lorraine a ride home."

While they were sitting in the jeep, a rotund little man with pale skin and a turned-up nose walked off the ferry, wearing an ill-fitting brown suit and carrying a bulky leather valise. He waited on the pier until a motorcycle with a sidecar came off the boat. The motorcycle driver appeared to be a tall woman wearing black leather pants and a jacket, with boots and a black leather cap with goggles pushed above the visor.

"That pair doesn't look like tourists to me," Lorraine said when the driver dismounted to help the odd little man get into the sidecar.

"It takes all kinds," Rossi said. "You never know."

The Rest of the Story

Connor and Bertram drove across the Mount Hope Bridge to Bristol after they spoke with Sergei, but Connor walked into the Rhode Island Veteran's Home by himself—Bertram had elected to wait outside—and he found Cole Lonsdale alone in his hospital bed, hooked up to an IV machine and staring at the ceiling.

"Hello, Mister Lonsdale, I'm Connor Laird. My wife met you yesterday and I thought I should come by myself and thank you for your service. How are you feeling today?"

"Good days, bad days, you know," Lonsdale said without looking at Connor. "Today is not so good. My insides are rotten."

"I'm sorry to hear that," Connor said. "You have one hell of a good story to tell."

"Yes, I've told it lots of times," Lonsdale said. "You can read about it in the newspapers."

"Sure," Connor said, "but I'd like to talk veteran-to-veteran, so you can tell the things you never could say to reporters."

Lonsdale raised his head to look at Connor and said, "You're a vet?"

"Yes," Connor said. "I was a Navy aviator in the final bombing campaign against North Vietnam, so I know how mixed-up things can get in wartime."

"Navy, huh?" Lonsdale said. "You know what we used to say? We'd say that the Coast Guard was the nucleus that the Navy forms around in time of war."

"I'm sure that's true," Connor said with a chuckle. "How did you get assigned to the mounted beach patrol?"

"I used to ride horses and work in the stables at Lincoln Woods as a kid," Lonsdale said. When I joined the Coast Guard, I wanted to drive a landing craft in the Pacific, or maybe pull convoy duty in the Atlantic. But when they saw I knew about horses, I got sent to Maryland for beach patrol training, then right back to Rhode Island."

"You're lucky," Connor said. "A lot of the Coast Guardsmen on landing crafts and convoy duty never came home."

"I know," Lonsdale said. "But I didn't miss out on the war—I got my Nazi on Block Island."

"You sure did," Connor said. "Why don't you tell me about the night you caught up with your Nazi? You saw him come ashore on the west side of the island, didn't you?"

"No," Lonsdale said, looking at the ceiling. "I'm tired of telling that story. That isn't what happened at all."

"That's okay," Connor said. "I know how messed up war is. Why don't you tell me what really happened?"

"Do you really want to know?" Lonsdale said. "I was taking a shortcut."

"You mean you were off your assigned patrol route?"

"It was foggy and dark," Lonsdale said. "You couldn't see a damn thing—it was no night to be stumbling around on the bluffs, that's for sure."

"Didn't you carry a Detex watchman's clock?" Connor said. "I thought they had keys mounted at places along your patrol route that were used to record the time you passed?"

"Yes, they had the keys on concrete pillars along the beach," Lonsdale said. "But we had run out of the paper discs that went in the clock, so we kept using the old ones over and over. Nobody could notice if one or two stations were missed now and then."

"So," Connor said, "you didn't actually see the man come ashore?"

"No," Lonsdale said. "I didn't see him until I was cutting across the island to the east side on Cooneymus Road."

"I understand," Connor said. "You had to make up a cover story to explain why you were inland and not on the beach along the south side that night."

"That's right," Lonsdale said. "But everybody knew the Nazis would come ashore at Dorie's Cove. It's the only place to get onto the island without being spotted and without climbing the bluffs. I figure that bugger had finished his reconnaissance and he was heading back to the cove on the west side to be picked up by the U-boat."

"So you didn't follow him inland at all?" Connor said. "He was actually walking west on Cooneymus Road, toward you, when you first saw him. Is that right?"

"It happened very fast," Lonsdale said. "You want to know something else? I never meant to shoot that man, even if he was a Nazi saboteur. I never meant to shoot anybody—it all just happened so fast."

"That's okay," Connor said. "You did what you had to do."

"No, you don't understand," Lonsdale said. "My horse reared—Cheyenne always was a bit skittish—and my rifle went off by accident. So, I had to say that the man was coming at me with that knife."

"I do understand," Connor said. "Screwy things happen in wartime. Did the man say anything that night?"

"I can't remember his exact words," Lonsdale said, "only that he called me 'friend' when we met. I didn't mean to shoot him, but everybody made such a big deal about the whole thing and when I went home to Pawtucket after the war, they wanted me to march in parades. What else could I do?"

Words

"I don't want to leave you," Betsy's sister said as the women had coffee on the patio outside the Drake house on an unusually warm and pleasant morning for Block Island in May. "But I must get home for Arthur's graduation."

"I'll be fine," Betsy said. "And Lorraine will come out to stay with me when she can."

"I will," Lorraine said. "And Becky, Connor will be happy to fly you on and off the island if you don't want to take the ferry."

"That's very generous," Becky said. "But it's so convenient to park my car in Point Judith and hop on the boat."

With that said and the coffeepot empty, the women got into the Woody and drove to the ferry landing, where the sisters went into the terminal to purchase Becky's ticket.

"I'll wait out here," Lorraine said when she saw Hattie's van nearby, waiting to pick up fares. The parking lot was abuzz with activity and the *Metacomet* was coming into the channel when she walked over to the driver's side window and said, "Hello, Hattie."

"Oh, hello," Hattie said. "I see the sister is leaving. Will you be staying?"

"I'll be back and forth," Lorraine said. "But tell me something, Hattie—I wonder—since you talk to so many people every day, have you ever heard any rumblings about Rusty straying?"

"Straying?" Hattie said. "Oh, you must mean the affair? Well—everybody knows about that."

"What do they know, Hattie?"

"Well, I'm not one to repeat this sort of scatter, but I did hear that he was seeing that Montgomery woman. Of course, with Dalton and Betsy off the island so often, it was only natural. They didn't even try to hide it that much the way they were seen together when their spouses were off-island. Of course Emily is one of those glamorous Hollywood types with their loose morals and all, and Rusty needed to be with his own kind. It had to happen."

"Are you talking about Dalton's wife?" Lorraine said, keeping her voice low enough that people walking by would not hear her words. "Emily Montgomery?"

"Everybody knows it," Hattie said. "Of course it's only natural that Rusty would want to be with his own kind. That's the way the Good Lord intended it, I'd say."

"His own kind?" Lorraine said. "What does that mean?"

"Well, of course—Betsy is a Jewess. Don't you know her maiden name—Feldman?"

"I see," Lorraine said, recoiling when Hattie's words hit her. "But you must know that most people don't care about that nonsense."

"Oh, it's not nonsense at all," Hattie said. "It even says so in the Bible, where it commands us to 'bring forth after our kind.' It's a trespass against God to take a strange wife."

"You're right," Lorraine said. "It's not simply nonsense—those words are full of hurt, Hattie. I hate to hear them."

"Oh, I'm not being mean," Hattie said. "It's a good thing Rusty never had children by Betsy. Well, I tell you, with Rusty being a direct descendant of Sir Francis Drake and all that, it would have been a crime against nature to contaminate that noble bloodline with Jew blood."

"Hattie, I'm too stunned to have this conversation here," Lorraine said as she backed away from the van, with people walking by. "Your words are so wrong on so many levels that I can't wrap my mind around them. All I ask is that you not repeat anything you might have heard about my friends."

"Oh, I didn't repeat that scatter," Hattie said. "You asked."

"Yes, I did," Lorraine said. "And I'll regret it forever."

Logan

Garcia and Rossi had lunch at Dead Eye Dick's and then went back to Rossi's office, where Garcia opened his laptop computer and logged on to the FBI server. He had been feeding the analyst at the Providence FBI office the names and relevant information of each actor in his investigation, and her report was an eye-opener.

"Rossi, you're going to love this," Garcia said. "Your traffic stop of Honey really paid off. Michelle Valentine is a known associate of two con men named Dirk Novak and—get this—Larry Logan, alias Logan Lawrence."

"You never know," Rossi said. "If he's not a Boston lawyer, what is Logan's game?"

"He's just a sleazy guy with a bag full of get-rich-quick schemes," Garcia said. "Lost gold mines, classic cars in South American sinkholes, woolly mammoth DNA from a glacier—whatever high-net-worth suckers want to throw some money at. But he really hit the jackpot with his latest scam—a hot tip on the coordinates of a lost atomic bomb in the Savannah River."

"You're kidding me," Rossi said. "Who would fall for that line of crap?"

"Apparently a few high rollers took the hook," Garcia said. "It seems that the Air Force actually did lose something off a B-47 in 1958, when the bomber had a midair collision with an F-86 fighter during a training exercise. It might have been a Mark 15 atomic bomb—but the plutonium core was not installed."

"Right," Rossi said. "I find it hard to believe that the Air Force would leave an armed A-bomb lying around."

"Exactly," Garcia said. "Except that congressional testimony by some dopey assistant secretary of defense—who didn't have a real grasp of the subject—hinted that the lost bomb was fully armed and lost somewhere near Tybee Island. The conspiracy crew had a field day with that misstatement, even though the Air Force countered with ample proof that there was nothing but a lead plug in the nose of that bomb."

"People believe what they want to believe," Rossi said. "You never know."

"True," Garcia said. "Logan isn't the first scammer to lead people down that rabbit hole, but he is one of the best. His investors have sunk millions into his search, hoping to claim salvage rights and ransom the bomb back to the Air Force."

"So what is he doing on my island?" Rossi said. "He's been renting that house for two years—and Honey has been off the island a few times—but he hardly ever goes outside the house."

"Logan has a big problem," Garcia said. "Usually his investors write off their losses, but this time he snookered some Malaysian billionaire, and this guy isn't going to sue Logan when he comes up short—he's going to kill him."

"Now I get the picture," Rossi said. "Is there any paper out for Logan and Dirk?"

"No warrants yet," Garcia said. "Only a slew of civil actions."

"Let's go have a talk with Logan anyway," Rossi said. "I hate it when people lie to me."

"Right," Garcia said, taking his .45 from his backpack and pushing it into his belt against his back. "Now we're getting somewhere."

Dirk

Connor flew the Widgeon out to Block Island in the afternoon, and Lorraine borrowed the Woody station wagon from Betsy to pick him up at the airport.

"What's all this?" Lorraine said as Connor took his dive gear from the airplane and loaded it into the Woody. "Are you really going to make a night dive to the U-853?"

"Sure," Connor said. "I'll get Tony to take me and Garcia out tonight."

"Dirk and his boys might not like that."

"They'll never know we were out there," Connor said as he covered the dive gear with a heavy wool blanket. "We'll push off at zero-three-thirty, and by the time they crawl out of bed the *Racketeer* will be tied up back at the dock."

"I don't like it," Lorraine said as she drove the Woody into town. "There's too much current in Rhode Island Sound, not to mention great white sharks this time of year. And you've never dived with Rene so you have no idea how he might react to trouble."

"I'm not worried about Garcia," Connor said. "He'll stay cool and do the same thing I would do in a tight spot."

"Maybe, but diving a hundred feet down at night is like visiting another world," Lorraine said. "And you're no spring chicken, Fly-boy."

"Hey, don't worry about me," Connor said. "I'm in great shape for a guy my age."

"You're doing okay, Connor," Lorraine said. "But Rene is younger and more athletic. Why not let him make the dive tomorrow with the state police dive team? They're professionals, after all."

"Back up," Connor said. "Garcia might be younger than me—but what do you mean by more athletic?"

"Take it easy, Fly-boy," Lorraine said. "You were very much the dashing Navy fighter pilot when we first met, but you've been sitting on your butt in airliners and pushing buttons for a long time now. Sometimes I worry that you still want to act like a sailor on liberty in Hong Kong."

"You really know how to hurt a guy," Connor said. "Have you had supper yet? I'm starved, and I saw the *Racketeer* headed into Old Harbor as I flew by. If we go to Ballard's, we might see them tie up at the dock."

Lorraine drove onto the dock and they arrived in time to watch Tony shift the rudder and propellers to walk the *Racketeer* sideways into a tight berth between two sailboats. When Connor saw that Dirk had his right arm in a sling, he got out of the Woody to get a closer look.

"What happened here?" Connor said.

"My passenger didn't have his sea legs today," Tony said, with a shrug.

"It's my damn shoulder," Dirk said. "I must have screwed up my rotator cuff again. I need to get to a hospital."

"There's no hospital on the island," Connor said. "So you have three choices—you can go across to the mainland by boat or you can wait for the next New England Airways flight to Westerly."

"That's only two choices," Dirk said.

"Right," Connor said. "Or you can fly to Newport with me right now."

"Wait a minute," Dirk said, "I know you—you're the guy with that crappy old airplane who met us at the airport."

"My Widgeon didn't get old by being a crappy airplane," Connor said. "And it'll cost you two hundred and fifty bucks to fly on it—cash, up front."

"Oh come on," Dirk said. "I don't carry cash, only credit cards. Can't you cut a guy a break? I'm in pain here."

"Those Lycoming engines don't run on good intentions," Connor said. "They gulp high-octane fuel—so it's up to you, pal."

"Okay," Dirk said, as he and the other divers rummaged through their bags to come up with the cash, which he handed to Connor.

"Right," Connor said. "Grab your gear—I'll carry your bag if your arm isn't up to it—and get into the car. My wife will drive us to the airport."

While Lorraine was helping Dirk into the Woody, Connor turned back to the *Racketeer* for a moment and spoke to Tony as he made up the bow line.

"Tony, I need a favor," he said. "I need to take a look at the U-853 myself. We'll push off at zero-three-thirty, while these two knuckleheads are sleeping in the hotel."

"You're going to dive alone?" Tony said. "At night?"

"No, Garcia has my back," Connor said. "You better get some shuteye—it's going to be a long night."

"No problem," Tony said. "I'll be ready."

Connor got into the backseat of the Woody and asked Dirk about having a taxi meet them at the airport in Newport as transportation to the hospital.

"No, I can get a ride from a friend," Dirk said, but he had some difficulty making a call on his cell phone with one hand.

"Allow me," Lorraine said, taking his cell phone in her own hands. Then she read the number off a slip of paper that Dirk held as she tapped the keys.

"Thanks," Dirk said when he took the phone back. Then he said, "Hey," into the phone, "I'm flying to Newport, right now. Come get me at the airport.... Yeah, it's my shoulder again... No, just be there quick as you can. Bye."

Not much was said as Lorraine drove them to the airport with Dirk riding shotgun in the front seat of the Woody. In the meantime Connor sat in the backseat and discreetly unzipped the gym bag that he had carried for Dirk. He wasn't surprised to find a large semiautomatic pistol—a chrome 10mm Sig Sauer with pearl grips—which he took from the bag and slipped under the front seat, out of sight.

The airport lineman opened the gate so that Lorraine could drive the Woody close to the Widgeon and Connor tossed Dirk's bag—without his pistol—onto the rearmost seat in the passenger compartment. He helped his passenger up the boarding ladder and then Connor said, "Can you make it to the right front seat on your own? Good, I'll be right there."

"I'll be back late tonight," Connor said to Lorraine, leaning into the Woody after Dirk was well out of earshot. "I'm going to have Rossi pick me up and I'll go straight to the police station with him to get ready for the dive with Garcia."

"I wish you would reconsider that dive," Lorraine said. "I have a bad feeling about it."

"We'll be all right," Connor said. "By the way, there's a big semiauto pistol under your seat—it's loaded—so don't touch it. Let Rossi handle it."

"How do I explain that?"

Connor said, "Just say that Dirk's carry-on bag didn't pass my preboarding inspection."

Then he climbed into the Widgeon and pulled the boarding ladder up before he closed the hatch and duck-walked to the cockpit, where Dirk had taken the copilot's seat. Before Connor took the pilot's seat, he pulled his own .45 auto out from under his sweatshirt and slipped it into a pouch on the sidewall near his left knee.

"You carry a gun?" Dirk said. "Man, are you hard-core, or what?"

"Call it what you want," Connor said as he started the engines. "I prefer to think of myself as old school."

Connor taxied the Widgeon to the runway and took off to the east and then turned north so that Old Harbor was under the left wing when they climbed away.

"Yeah, I remember how you talked all tough at the airport that day," Dirk said, when the Widgeon was over open water. "So if you're so 'old school,' how did you lose the war in Vietnam?"

"I delivered my ordinance on target and returned to the ship after every mission," Connor said. "When the other side was ready to negotiate, I came home to my family in the most prosperous nation on earth. Do you call that losing?"

Connor flew over the water at only two thousand feet, and within ten minutes they were circling down to land on runway 22 at Newport, where he rolled the wheels onto the asphalt and rumbled up to the terminal.

"Don't forget your bag," Connor said after he opened the hatch and put the boarding ladder out.

"There's my ride," Dirk said as a dirty and dented Bavarian sedan pulled up with a blonde woman behind the wheel. When he reached for the door handle to jump into the passenger seat of the BMW, it seemed that his shoulder had made a remarkable recovery.

"You're welcome," Connor said as the car quickly sped away.

Logan

Rossi and Garcia went to the south side of the island and drove up the narrow dirt path to the rented house where Larry Logan—aka attorney Logan Lawrence—was living.

"What do you want now?" Logan said when he opened the door to the house.

"We'd like to come in and ask you a few questions," Rossi said.

"Questions about what?"

"We're interested in what you might have seen or heard at the Dodge farm next door around the time that Rusty Drake went missing."

"No, you can't come in," Logan said, standing in his open doorway. "I never really met that guy and I didn't see anything. I'm working on a complex business proposal and you're just wasting my time."

"What guy is that?" Rossi said.

"That farmer guy next door," the man said. "He's got nothing to do with me."

Then Garcia said, "I'm Special Agent Garcia of the Federal Bureau of Investigation. Is your name Larry Logan?"

"Crap, haven't you got better things to do?"

"Before you answer my questions," Garcia said, "you should know that making false statements during an FBI interview is a felony under Title 18 of the United States Code."

"Yeah, I know," Logan said. "I went to law school, even if I never passed the bar exam."

"So," Garcia said, "were you born on March 5, 1974?"

"Sure, that's me," Logan said. "But using an alias is a common business practice. And there's no law against saying I'm a lawyer as long as I didn't take money for legal advice or make a motion in court."

"You seem to have an idea of exactly how far you can push the truth," Garcia said. "Why don't you tell me about Sunrise Investments?"

"There's no problem there," Logan said. "My clients will get every penny back. It just takes time."

"Oh?" Garcia said. "I understand that some of your customers are taking legal action against you. Isn't one foreign investor very upset about his losses?"

"Look, I know how to handle those people," Logan said. "I'll take care of it."

While Garcia was talking to Logan, Rossi ventured to the side of the house, prompting Logan to say, "Where's he going?"

"Chief Rossi is looking around for officer safety," Garcia said. "I'd like to talk to Miss Valentine. When do you expect her to return?"

"I don't know," Logan said. "Her mother is sick in Brooklyn, so Honey has to go down and help her all the time. Now I have very important work to do, so why don't you leave me alone?"

"Does this important business concern the U-853?" Garcia said.

"You bet it does," Logan said. "And I'm well within my rights to explore that wreck."

"That wreck has been declared a National Marine Sanctuary," Garcia said. "You can look, but any attempt to disturb the remains of the crew is inexcusable."

"I don't give a damn about those bones," Logan said. "I have important business on that submarine, and I'll tell you something else—I have friends in Washington who look out for me—very powerful friends."

Rossi had gone all around the house by then and he came back to stand alongside Garcia without saying a word.

"Are you threatening me, Mister Logan?" Garcia said.

"No, that's just a fact," Logan said as he closed the door. "Now leave me alone."

The two lawmen were walking away when Rossi said, "That sounded like a threat to me."

"Right," Garcia said. "Isn't that how we know we're getting close to busting a suspect? That 'powerful friends' line is the last-ditch effort to throw us off the trail—and it's always bullshit. Did you see anything interesting around the yard?"

"Yes," Rossi said, as they drove away.

Garcia said, "Well—?

"It's your turn to love this," Rossi said. "I saw tracks leading up to the bulkhead door to the basement—tractor tire tracks."

The Bund

Connor refueled the Widgeon after his flight from the island and called Lorraine soon after Dirk and his companion drove away from the Newport Airport. Her voice sounded somewhat different—more subdued—on his cell phone.

"That was Honey," Lorraine said after Connor described the BMW and the driver. "So those two are up to something on the mainland, just as we suspected."

"Maybe," Connor said. "Unless we just gave Dirk a means of escape."

"They won't get far," Lorraine said. "I wrote down Honey's phone number after I dialed the cell phone for Dirk. Garcia will be able to find them with that."

"Nice work there," Connor said. "What do you suppose they're up to?"

"I'm sure of one thing," Lorraine said. "Whatever those lovebirds are doing, it involves double-crossing Logan."

"You're right about that," Connor said. "Anyway, I'm going home to have dinner and take a nap. Rossi is going to pick me up at the airport on the island after midnight, so I probably won't see you until tomorrow."

Then Connor drove home to their house on Catherine Street. By then Bennett had been home from school for about two hours, and he greeted his father with a question.

"Hey, Dad," Bennett said. "Did you take some of my dive gear to the island today?"

"I did," Connor said. "Garcia needs to borrow some of your stuff. He and I are going down to the U-853 tonight."

"And you're not taking me?" Bennett said. "You told me I could go down to the U-boat someday."

"This isn't the time for that, Ben. Not by a long shot. Let's go inside and eat."

Bennett had prepared dinner—pork chops, sautéed vegetables, and potatoes—and they sat with Bertram at the small table in the breakfast nook to eat.

"As you requested," the old ambassador said as he cut a chop and speared a piece with his fork, "I've been reading about the aviatrix Laura Houghtaling Ingalls. I suppose you know that she was from a wealthy Brooklyn family descended from the original German settlers of New Amsterdam—her brother married J.P. Morgan's granddaughter—and that wealth gave her the freedom to buy the finest airplanes of the era."

"That's right," Connor said. "Then she used those airplanes to perform sensational but meaningless stunts that appealed to the public and the Guinness Book of Records people, but did not impress pilots in the least."

"Of course this was the depression era," Bertram said, "when dance marathons and flagpole sitting were all the rage. But it was also the era of the America First Committee, when many Americans wanted to stay out of a war that was persecuting Jews all over Europe with extreme prejudice, so there was always a strong undercurrent of anti-Semitism in this move-ment. Laura Ingalls was a favorite orator at their rallies, using incendiary rhetoric that was charged with hyperbole and Nazi salutes. So it became quite an embarrassment to the committee when an FBI indictment revealed that a German embassy official—actually the head of the Gestapo in America—had been feeding her Nazi propaganda and paying her three hundred dollars a month, which was a considerable sum at the time. As a result she became one of the first people prosecuted under the Foreign Agents Registration Act, or FARA. I believe that she served less than two years in prison, and then went right back to lobbying for Hitler. She was arrested again near the end of the war trying to enter Mexico with a suitcase full of seditious material, like recordings of Tokyo Rose radio broadcasts from Japan, but was not prosecuted. By then the FBI had decided that she was just a quack, and not worth their time."

"Grandpa," Bennett said, "how do you know all this stuff?"

"I was there," Bertram said. "I was the same age as you—seventeen years old—when America entered the war. I recall seeing the newsreels of the German American Bund rally in Madison Square Garden in 1939 where twenty thousand people cheered as their leader—a fiery little man dressed in riding britches and a Sam Browne belt, just like Hitler—decried Franklin Delano Roosevelt's New Deal as the 'Jew Deal.' There were banners and brown-shirt storm troopers chanting 'Will and Might' and 'Blood and Soil' and all that ethnic-nationalist nonsense."

"I can't believe that Americans would act that way," Bennett said.

"Unfortunately the Bund was not taken seriously by most of us," Bertram said. "For the most part they were laughed at."

"Didn't Meir Lansky's gang scuffle with the Nazis the night of their big rally?" Connor said.

"The Jewish Mafia beat the devil out of the Bund at every opportunity," Bertram said. "And Walter Winchell railed against them on the radio nearly every day."

"Is that what ended the Bund?" Bennett said.

"No," Bertram said as he finished his meal. "The Bund rotted from the inside. You see, fascist groups are based on the adoration of the strong man—the one man who can get things done—the leader's will is the law and the law is the leader's will. In the case of the Bund their *Furher*—Fritz Kuhn—was as corrupt and morally bankrupt as their so-called ideology of hate and exclusion. In the end, the Bund members rejected Kuhn and Americans rejected the Bund."

"Not before Hitler's gang had what they needed," Connor said. "The Bund gave the Gestapo a large list of Nazi sympathizers in America."

"You are absolutely correct," Bertram said. "The Bund simply went underground. Unfortunately, those ethnic-nationalist sentiments are present in our society to this day, just beneath the surface. Consider that the American Nazi Party actually had their headquarters in Arlington, Virginia, until 1983 when they changed their name to The New Order and dispersed to Michigan and Wisconsin."

"What was it Santayana said?" Connor said. "Those who cannot remember the past are condemned to repeat it."

Sweet Revenge

Garcia was sitting near the window in his hotel room later that afternoon when a soft knock came on the door. He had his pistol in hand when he answered the tapping, but he tucked the cold steel into his waistband when he found Lorraine in the hallway.

"Come on in," he said. "I thought you flew to the mainland with Connor."

"No." Lorraine said as she walked deep into the room. "I was going to stay with Betsy, but she and Rossi had a lot to talk about, so when he came to the house I decided to borrow the Woody and go for a ride around the island." She was wearing a light blue sweater and white Bermuda shorts when she turned in the middle of the room to face him and said, "So, here I am."

"Good," Garcia said. "We can get some dinner. When is Connor coming back?"

"Rossi is supposed to pick him up at the airport after midnight," Lorraine said. The window was open and a gentle breeze was ruffling the lace curtains and she went to it. The *Racketeer* was tied to the dock across the harbor and when she put her forearms on the windowsill to look out, she said, "You've been spying, haven't you?"

"We call it surveillance, not spying," Garcia said, standing alongside her. Then he leaned on the windowsill with their shoulders touching and said, "Lorraine, what do you really want to talk about?"

"Rene, don't go diving with Connor tonight," she said, turning on one elbow to face him. "Talk him out of it—you're the only one he will listen to."

"Nobody can change Connor's mind," Garcia said. "Like his decision to give Dirk an easy way off the island—I wish he hadn't done that without talking to me."

"Yes, that might have been a mistake," Lorraine said. "Apparently Honey met him in Newport, after which it seems that Dirk's shoulder injury made a dramatic recovery."

"No surprise there," Garcia said. "But it shouldn't be hard to locate both of them after we figure out what crimes they were involved in."

"When will that be?"

"Soon," Garcia said. "Our night dive to the U-853 might tell us most of the story."

"Well—" Lorraine said, touching his arm. "I don't know—I just don't feel good about this dive."

"We'll be fine," he said. "It's going to be a spike dive—get down quick, spend two minutes on the bottom, and then make a controlled ascent. There will be two scuba bottles with regulators hanging under the *Racketeer* so we can do a decompression stage on the way up—fifteen minutes at fifteen feet."

"You've never dived together before," Lorraine said.

"That's the last thing to worry about," Garcia said. "Connor and I have been in some tough situations—you can tell a lot about a man when you're taking fire from deadly opponents—you know that."

"Which is why I'm sure that Connor told you all about Leona," she said. "I know that he cheated with her in Mexico."

"Why would he tell me about that?" Garcia said.

"Men love to share the tales of their exploits," she said. "The night of the volcano, when he went hunting for the Russian with Leona—he must have given you all the juicy details."

"I don't know," Garcia said. "Maybe something happened in Leona's truck, but there was another truck full of her *pistoleros* standing guard, so those were not normal times."

"So you do know."

"That's between you and Connor," Garcia said. "Don't drag me into this."

"You're already in," Lorraine said. She touched the stubble of a beard on his cheek, and she said, "This morning-after look suits you, Rene."

"How is that?"

"I like it," she said. "You look—dangerous."

"I wouldn't think you'd like a beard," Garcia said. "Connor is always clean-shaven."

"Yes, and he shines his shoes every morning and gives himself a short haircut with the clippers every week. But let's not talk about him," Lorraine said, with her hands on his shoulders. He raised his arms when she pulled his shirt over his head, and she said, "It's my turn for sweet revenge with an exciting younger man—a very exciting man."

There was no finesse when they came together, kissing hard, pulling her clothes off—her scent captivated him and roused his passion. He picked her up and dropped her on the bed and ripped the buttons on her shirt while she was still pulling her sweater off.

"This is tonight," Lorraine said, gasping for air. "It's all over once we go out that door."

"Whatever you say."

Revenge was sudden, exciting, and sweet.

7

Friday, May 13

A Trick at The Wheel

Connor flew back to Block Island above a wispy veil of fog that was clinging to the water of Rhode Island Sound, illuminated by the silver glow of a full moon. But the airport was clear when he landed, well after midnight. Rossi was waiting for him, so he loaded the dive gear into Rossi's jeep and they went to the police station, where Connor napped in one of the jail cells for a few hours. Then Rossi drove him to Old Harbor, where Tony was waiting at the dock with the *Racketeer*'s engines idling. It was three o'clock in the morning and two small fishing boats were already leaving the harbor to trawl for the catch of the day for the fish market and the island's restaurants.

"It's about time," Connor said when Garcia came walking from the National Hotel just in time to help take their diving equipment from Rossi's jeep and put it onto the *Racketeer*.

"Good morning to you too," Garcia said.

Then Connor pointed to some deep scrapes on the boat's deck and he said, "Captain Tony, what happened here?"

"Those jokers brought some real heavy stuff aboard yesterday," Tony said. "They're making a mess of the *Racketeer*, but there's a pot of hot coffee in the galley for you gents—help yourselves."

Rossi and Garcia went below while Connor helped cast off the mooring lines. Then he stood next to Tony with a cup of coffee while the captain walked the *Racketeer* sideways off the dock and headed out of the channel. The water was perfectly calm except for the ripples of the boat's wake as the harbor lights faded astern. The rocks of the breakwater soon disappeared in the fog and darkness ahead of them, but the beacon light on the end of the jetty shone through the mist like a guiding star until they passed it close to starboard and Captain Tony turned the *Racketeer* out to sea.

"I'll take a cup of that joe now," Tony said when the lights of Block Island were nothing more than a memory. "You want to take a trick at the wheel, Connor?"

"Sure," Connor said. "What's the heading?"

"East by a quarter north," Tony said. "And try not to hit anything, okay?"

"Can you give me that in degrees?" Connor said.

"What?" Tony said. "Have you been navigating up in the clouds so long you don't remember how to steer by a nautical compass? That's eighty-seven degrees to a fly-boy—or a landlubber."

"Eighty-seven degrees, aye," Connor said. "Shouldn't we turn on the radar?"

"That son of a bitch don't work," Tony said. "Soon as I get paid for this charter I'm putting a Furuno radar on the boat. You can't beat those Jap electronics."

"Right," Connor said. "It's always something with a boat, isn't it?"

"Ain't that the truth," Tony said. "Why did you sell your boat anyway, Connor? The *Bolter* was a beautiful old sailboat. I always like seeing her running in a fresh breeze with a bone in her teeth."

"She was wood and she was too high maintenance," Connor said. "That, and it was just a bad time in my life."

"That's too bad," Tony said. "But I know all about bad times myself. After Marco died I didn't want to see a boat for a long time."

"Right," Connor said. "Losing a son has to be the worst thing that can happen to a man. But what happened? Did Marco really fall overboard?"

"Hell no," Tony said. "He was gone before he hit the water. I even know who did it, but I promised Donna I wouldn't get revenge, because she didn't want to end up alone with me in prison. Anyway, Dante Colasanto was supposed to take care of those guys—Marco was working for him—but he wouldn't make the hit. That's why I don't talk to him or his crew anymore."

"That sucks," Connor said. "There's no other way to say it—it just sucks."

Then nothing was said for a time while the two men held to their own thoughts and listened to the sounds of the engines and the waves slapping the hull.

"Wait a minute," Connor finally said, when the sound of a distant foghorn came through the fog. "Did you hear that?"

"Yup, there's something big out there," Tony said. "Let's slow down, Connor. Just maintain steerageway until it goes by."

When Connor pulled the throttles back to idle, Rossi and Garcia came up from the cabin to see what was going on. They arrived on deck just in time to see the running lights and shadowy form of a giant ship pass close ahead of the *Racketeer*.

"That's the *Marine Electric*," Tony said, recognizing the dark outline of the vessel with a large conveyor track amidships for unloading coal. "She makes a regular run to deliver coal to the power station at Brayton Point up by Fall River."

"I wouldn't want to get in the way of a ship that big," Rossi said.

"Neither would I," Tony said. "But we're only about a half-mile from the U-boat, so you boys might as well stay on deck. We wrapped an anchor line around the conning tower with a buoy on the surface, so all you have to do is grab the marker buoy and make the anchor line fast to that cleat on the bow when I say so."

Twenty Fathoms

The night was dark and the sea was calm when Connor rolled off the side of the *Racketeer* and splashed into the underwater world, where he hovered weightlessly a few feet below the surface and waited for Garcia to follow. You can tell everything you need to know about a diver by how they get into the water, so Connor was relieved to see that his dive partner also dropped in with no awkward splashing or last-minute adjustments at the surface.

They had hung two scuba bottles with regulators fifteen feet beneath the boat so they could pause there to decompress when they were returning to the surface at the end of the dive, and Connor paused just long enough to inspect each one of them.

This will work, Connor thought as he put his head down and started kicking his fins to descend quickly down the anchor line. Each inhalation hissed through the regulator in his mouth and bubbled up toward the surface as he exhaled: *Sssss—bub-bub-bubble.* Any sound that reached his ears was muted and distant, and the water beyond the beam of his flashlight was a black void. *Ssssssss—bub-bub-bub-bubble.* The hulk of the U-853 came into view suddenly—sitting upright on the bottom with gaping holes blasted through the hull—and Connor slowed his descent to hang on the anchor line alongside the conning tower.

Ssss—bub-bubble.

Garcia appeared alongside him a moment later with a thumbs-up. Connor was happy to see that he wasn't too excited—as long as they were both sipping air and making small bubbles they would have the necessary bottom time to get a good look at the wreck—and maybe figure out what mischief Dirk's divers were up to.

Connor kicked and swam toward the stern of the wreck, with Garcia close behind and both men shining their powerful flashlights on the crusted and broken remains of the once-fearsome German war machine. The wood decking that had once covered the thick steel of the pressure hull, as well as the thin steel fairings and railings, had eroded away years earlier. Sand and mud were filling the hull, which was broken and split in a half-dozen places—exposing the pipes and machinery within—and every surface was festooned with barnacles and purple and white sea anemones.

The men rounded the stern and kicked their flippers to swim toward the bow on the starboard side. There was a gaping hole forward of the conning tower where a depth charge had landed on deck and exploded while the submarine was lying on the bottom, presumably hoping to avoid detection. The sea had arranged a funeral bouquet of white anemones on yellow stalks like flowers around a hatch where human femur bones were visible.

The wreck looked unchanged to Connor until they swam near the bow, which had been fairly blown off during the bombardment in 1945, where he noticed many polypropylene ropes tied to the wreck, all bright yellow and untarnished by the sea. These were new—and in the beam of his flashlight he saw something disturbing—something lying on the seafloor alongside the wreck—that had not been there before.

Connor motioned for Garcia to stay up at the level of the submarine's deck when he went down to the seafloor alongside the bow, descending to just over 120 feet—which was certainly deeper than he had intended to go. But there on the bottom were four pieces of cylindrical tanks and a maze of tubing and wiring—and it struck Conner in a moment of recognition—*that's what's left of a torpedo!*

Sssssss—bub-bub-bubble-bub-bubble.

The casing of the torpedo had mostly rusted away, but there were places where the metal was almost bright from being recently cut and torn apart—*this was the work of hydraulic shears,* Connor thought, *just like the ones we saw being loaded into the Hummer at the airport.*

There was also a new hole in the pressure hull of the U-853—just large enough to pull a torpedo out, in pieces—and Connor shined his light inside, where he saw a tangle of wreckage. But there was something else inside the submarine—something inside a small cavity within the pressure hull. Something he would have to place himself partially inside to reach.

Sssss—bub-bubble.

Connor reached his arms forward and eased his head and torso into the hole, almost touching the object before half a century of silt billowed up inside the broken hull. Immediately the water around him turned into an opaque, swirling Slurpee of brown mud that his flashlight could not penetrate. Only when he got his facemask against the object did he realize that it was the warhead off the dismantled torpedo that was lying on the seafloor outside. Some things had been placed under the warhead, but he couldn't make out what the objects were.

Connor tried to back out of the hole, but he encountered resistance. He was blinded by the silt churning in the water and hung up on something, and each movement made the swirling mud darker and more ominous. When his hand bumped against something, he was revolted to realize that it was a human skull that had been buried in the mud.

This is a hell of a way to go, Connor thought. *I'm already too deep and I'll run out of air before I untangle myself from this mess.*

Then Connor felt a tug at his leg—then a twist—and Garcia was pulling him out, guiding his air bottle and weight belt out through the hole.

Connor pointed upward, and the two men kicked toward the conning tower, where they began slowly ascending. They purposefully came up slower than their bubbles, allowing the gurgling silver airstream from their regulators to lead the way to the surface. They didn't look at their air pressure gauges since they knew they were almost out of air but they couldn't rise faster.

Connor's regulator made high-pitched sounds and stopped giving him air—the air bottle on his back was empty—just as they arrived at the spare bottles and regulators hanging fifteen feet under the *Racketeer*. They halted their ascent there and breathed off the spare bottles while they waited for the tiny nitrogen bubbles that had surely accumulated in their bloodstreams during the deep dive to dissipate, giving each other a reassuring thumbs-up all the while. *We're going to be okay.*

Ballard's

The *Racketeer* arrived back in the harbor before dawn, and Rossi brought Connor and Garcia straight to the police station with their dive gear. They took naps behind the bars in the holding cell while Rossi made his early morning round of the island before the three of them went to Ballard's for breakfast. By then Tony had already refueled the *Racketeer*, so Logan's divers would have no idea that his boat had made a secret trip to the U-853 hours earlier.

"So," Lorraine said when she and Betsy arrived for breakfast with the men. "What did you boys find on that old U-boat?"

"I'm not sure," Connor said. "It looks like they expanded a hole in the hull to get inside and chop a torpedo into pieces so they could drag it out—but why and what for, we have no idea."

"That sounds like a foolish thing to do," Betsy said. "What if the torpedo had exploded while they were cutting it?"

"They carefully avoided the warhead," Garcia said. "Which is a good thing, since the Germans used a highly explosive compound that could still be volatile—and extremely unstable—after six decades under salt water."

"That's a fact," Rossi said. "A few years ago a fishing trawler dragged up the front end of a rusty old torpedo that looked harmless, but when the ordnance disposal boys took it over to Sand Hill Cove and set off a small charge, the warhead exploded and blew a giant crater in the dunes. The blast blew out the windows of a dozen beach cottages and was heard loud and clear twenty miles away, so I have healthy respect for any old ordnance the fishermen drag up."

"You're making it sound like Logan's gang is planning to risk dragging that warhead out of the wreck," Betsy said. "But why? Do they know something that we don't know?"

"Maybe," Lorraine said. "What if that torpedo wasn't armed with conventional explosives?"

"What are you getting at?" Connor said. "The Germans never succeeded in making an A-bomb, if that's what you're thinking."

"Can you be sure of that?" Lorraine said. "Logan's company was supposedly looking for a big payday by finding an atomic bomb that the US Air Force had supposedly lost off the coast of Georgia—which you say was actually a training bomb with no nuclear warhead—so what if he's trying to stave off his investors with another wild-goose chase?"

"That's an interesting theory," Connor said. "I suppose a fairy tale about a Nazi atomic torpedo is no harder to swallow than some nonsense about one of our own lost A-bombs—even though it would have made no sense at all for the Nazis to attempt an atomic attack against us in May of 1945. The Russians were already in Berlin and the war in

Europe was a mopping-up operation by then. An attack like that would have pissed off the American public in a big way, and the result might have been very bad for post-war Germany."

"Uh-oh," Rossi said, nodding toward the parking lot, where a motorcycle with a sidecar was pulling in. "Let's be careful what we say now, our plump little friend may be coming in here."

"Let's invite him to our table," Lorraine said when the man came in the door. "We're going to have to talk to him sooner or later."

"We don't have time for that right now," Garcia said as the man waddled into Ballard's and took a seat at the far side of the dining room. "He's a bit eccentric, for sure, but he hasn't done anything suspicious yet."

"I don't know about that," Betsy said. "It gives me the creeps—the way he's been driving around the island all day just looking at things and talking to people without saying anything about himself."

"I may have to resort to another traffic stop," Rossi said, looking to his driver, who had stayed outside and leaned against the motorcycle, reading a comic book. "I'm sure I could find some reason to pull that sidecar contraption over."

"Now, Brian," Betsy said, "did you really just say that you sometimes stop cars just to interrogate the driver?"

"Of course I do," Rossi said. "That's straight out of the cop handbook. We also look for suspicious items in plain sight."

"You'd be surprised how many major crimes get solved by a lucky traffic stop," Garcia said.

"Well," Lorraine said as the waitress brought their omelets and pancakes to the table. "I still think we should go ahead and talk to him."

"Don't you dare," Connor said, even though he knew that his admonition was falling on deaf ears.

They were done eating breakfast by the time the Hummer finally pulled onto the pier at eight o'clock, and no one was surprised to see the two divers carry some heavy diving equipment onto the *Racketeer*. But when Logan himself got out of the backseat and carried a black suitcase to the boat, Rossi said, "Here we go, boys and girls, the plot just thickened."

"Why do you say that?" Betsy said.

"Because Logan is going out to the U-853 for the first time—as far as we know—and that case contains a very fancy video camera. It was opened on the floor near the back windows when I did a sweep around his house last Sunday, and I could see some high-end gear inside."

"Right," Garcia said. "Logan is known to entice his investors with elaborate video presentations. Maybe something dramatic is going to be staged out there today."

"Damn it," Connor said when they heard the rumbling sound of the *Racketeer's* engines starting. "I shouldn't let Tony go out there with them by himself today—he didn't get any sleep last night."

"Too late now," Garcia said as they watched Tony walk the boat sideways off the dock and motor slowly out of the harbor.

"Listen, Betsy," Rossi said. "I have something to tell you. The state police are on their way to the island as we speak. The detectives are flying over and the rest of the troopers will be arriving on the morning ferry. We are going to conduct a very thorough investigation of J.D.'s farm."

"I see," Betsy said. "So, is that where you think—"

"We have to cover all the bases," Rossi said. "I hope you understand—it's just a possibility we'll find something there. You should go home and stay there—I'll let you know what happens as soon as I can."

"I do understand," Betsy said as they all watched the *Racketeer* cruise slowly along the breakwater and out of the harbor. "Nothing about that miserable little man will surprise me. Someone should have put J.D. out of his misery long ago."

The Portly Man

When the group went outside after breakfast, they found that the fog had cleared and that a beautiful sun-drenched morning had descended on Old Harbor. The men drove away in Rossi's police jeep but Lorraine and Betsy decided to take a stroll around the harbor to enjoy the sunshine, so when the portly man stomped out of Ballard's in his orthopedic shoes the women were waiting for him.

"Good morning sir," Lorraine said. "May we have a word with you?"

"By all means," he said. Several park benches faced the harbor, and he motioned to the one closest to the motorcycle and said, "Let's sit, shall we?"

His driver never looked up from her comic book when Lorraine and Betsy sat on either side of the man. When they were that close to him, they saw that his face was slightly chapped from the sun and wind, as if he was unaccustomed to the outdoors. But before the women could introduce themselves the man said, "Now I am truly a thorn between two very accomplished roses. You are the journalist Lorraine Calhoun Laird, are you not? I've enjoyed your writing, especially your recent dispatches concerning certain current and historic events on this island."

With a smile the man turned to Betsy and said, "And you are the photographer Betsy Drake, I believe? Let me say that I have enjoyed your work as well. And allow me to offer my condolences for the possible demise of your husband—I am truly sorry for your loss."

"You certainly know a great deal about us," Lorraine said. "Mister—?"

"Doctor," he said. "Doctor Louis Herman, from Milwaukee, Wisconsin."

"You didn't come all the way from Milwaukee in that sidecar?" Betsy said.

"Decidedly not. My niece lives in Provincetown, and I engaged her for local transportation during my visit. And I must say, jaunting around these narrow island roads in that sidecar has been an exhilarating experience."

The women turned to look at the niece when Doctor Herman mentioned her—

Something's not quite right here, Lorraine thought—and the niece casually nodded before planting her face back into the comic book.

"That's interesting," Lorraine said. "So, what brings you to Block Island all the way from the shores of Lake Michigan?"

"I was hoping someone would ask that," the doctor said with a smile. "You see, my hobby is hunting Nazis. I've spent years tracking certain party officials and other criminals who were not fully accounted for at the end of the war."

"Now I understand," Lorraine said. "All this activity around the U-853 must have aroused your curiosity."

THE RULES OF FATE

"Yes, I'm always watching the Associated Press and United Press International newswires for Nazi sightings and so forth, but these supposed enigmas of the Third Reich are almost always pure nonsense. However, I have long been interested in the mystery man—the so-called Tightrope Walker—who came ashore from the U-853, and I have followed every word written by Russell Drake on that matter. I must say, his articles were refreshing, clear of speculation and hyperbole."

"Thank you," Betsy said. "Russell would appreciate that."

"By the way," the doctor said, "is there any news of your husband?"

"No," Betsy said. "We may never know."

"I am so sorry," he said. "How shall I say this—if you will forgive my asking—do you suspect that his disappearance is in any way connected to the new activity on the U-853?"

"That's what we're trying to figure out," Lorraine said. "And frankly, your sudden appearance on the scene adds another layer of questions to the mystery. For instance, if you've been interested in the Tightrope Walker for so long, why did you choose this moment to come to this island?"

"That is a valid question," he said. "I never had any reason to doubt the official US Navy conclusion that the Tightrope Walker was an ordinary crewman from the U-853—until I read your article on the AP newswire this past Wednesday. One sentence in that article mentions that over the years many famous and infamous persons—including the aviatrix Laura Ingalls—had visited the island. That was my eureka moment!"

"I'm sorry," Lorraine said, "but there is no evidence that Ingalls was here on the island in May of 1945, so it seems unlikely that the Tightrope Walker was attempting to rendezvous with her."

"Ah! That's true," the doctor said. "But didn't you say that Ingalls stayed at the Wagner guest house for her visit?"

"I did," Lorraine said. "So—?"

"As you may know the Wagner guest house burned to the ground in 1961," the doctor said, signaling to his niece to bring something from the motorcycle. "But I was able to locate several old photographs."

"Thank you, Michelle," the doctor said when she handed him a black-and-white photograph, which he in turn passed to Lorraine.

"This photograph from the summer of 1937 is particularly illuminating, especially the sign."

Lorraine took the black-and-white print and held it so that Betsy could also look at it. The picture showed some people in old-fashioned bathing suits on the front porch of a house, and under the "Wagner Guest House" sign alongside the door was another sign that stated *Whites Only.*

"This doesn't seem remarkable to me," Lorraine said. "I would imagine that most—if not all—of the lodging on the island was segregated in 1937."

"Perhaps," the doctor said, as he produced a magnifying glass from his coat pocket and handed it to Lorraine. "But please look more closely at the sign."

When Lorraine studied the photograph under the magnifier, she saw that someone had added to the "Whites Only" sign—with smaller, crude brushstrokes—*No Jews.*

"It's disappointing to see that," Betsy said after she studied the sign with the magnifier. "I've always considered this pleasant little island to be a haven from that hate."

"I can't believe that was a common sentiment here," Lorraine said. "The Wagner family must have been an exception."

When Lorraine handed the photograph to the doctor's motorcycle driver, she noticed that Michelle's hands were large and strong, while his, when she returned the magnifier to him, were small and dainty.

"I must agree that the Wagners were stridently anti-Semitic," Doctor Herman said. "Which makes me believe that the Tightrope Walker was attempting to reach the Wagner home when he was killed by the beach patrol. I have no doubt that the purpose of Ingalls's visit in September was to lay the groundwork for his arrival."

"I'll have to think about that," Lorraine said. "Bigots have a way of finding each other in a dark room, so it may well be a coincidence that Ingalls stayed at Wagner's simply because Jews were excluded there. I know that she had been convicted of being a foreign agent and had spent a few months in prison, but is there any evidence that she was still communicating with Berlin at that stage of the war?"

"The first rule of hunting Nazis is that there are no such things as coincidences," the doctor said. "No, I believe that Wagner's was a way station on a sort of underground railroad—a ratline—for Nazis secretly arriving in North America. After a few days or weeks there, they could blend with other tourists on the island and take the ferry to the mainland without arousing suspicion."

"Then tell me, Doctor," Betsy said. "Who was the Tightrope Walker?"

"I can't say, exactly," the doctor said. "But I do believe that he was sent here on a mission—I am now quite certain that he arrived on these shores with a large cache of Nazi gold to be delivered to certain wealthy and influential supporters of the former America First Committee. Their goal—which would take many decades—was to create an all-powerful American National Socialist Party that could restore order and create an ethnically pure society in North America."

"That sounds…incredible," Lorraine said. "Of course, I'm a journalist and that would be the scoop of the century. So may I ask you what research you have done to arrive at this conclusion?"

"Well, I'm not married and I live above my practice, so I have a great deal of time to read and write letters of inquiry in my study. Luckily I am fluent in German."

Betsy said, "Your study?"

"Yes, I turned my spare bedroom into a sort of headquarters for my research. I have amassed such a great number of books and files over the years that they spill out into the hallway and the dining room, but it will all be worthwhile in the end."

"Doctor, have you traveled to Germany to do any research?" Lorraine said. "Have you studied the contemporary records in detail and have you conducted and documented interviews?"

"No, of course not. My work has been done in secret and in the privacy of my home, out of necessity. This is the first time I've actually had a lead worth traveling to investigate."

"I see," Lorraine said, with a sideways glance at Betsy. "And how would you propose to prove your theory?"

"When I find the gold, of course," the rotund man said, leaning forward to whisper. "It's still here on the island—you can be certain of that."

"What if the divers find the gold on the submarine?" Betsy said.

"They won't," he said. "The Tightrope Walker would not have let the treasure out of his sight and grasp for a moment—I suspect that he slept on top of it from the time he left Berlin. It is inconceivable that he came ashore here before the gold was safely stashed so that he could rendezvous with his patrons."

"I see," Lorraine said. "And where would you propose to look for a treasure that has been hidden on a small island for six decades?"

"Oh, I have several ideas," the portly doctor said. "Perhaps in a root cellar or a barn, or at the bottom of an old well—or under a pigsty—there are so many places, but I have a good idea where to look."

"Well, good luck with that," Lorraine said as she and Betsy stood up. They were walking to the Woody when she turned back to say, "By the way, sir, what sort of doctor are you?"

"I'm a podiatrist."

"Of course," Lorraine said, looking back at his orthopedic shoes. "I should have guessed that."

Grim Fate

When the men arrived at the airport, Connor went straight to the Widgeon while Rossi and Garcia waited for the helicopter carrying the state police detectives to land.

"Where are you going?" Rossi asked.

"I feel bad about letting Tony go out there with those knuckleheads by himself today," Connor said. "So, I'm going to go up and keep an eye on the *Racketeer* from the air."

"Nice move," Garcia said. "But you could be a real pal and stay here to root around in the mud at J.D.'s farm with us."

"No thanks," Connor said as he climbed aboard the amphibian. "I have a good idea what you're going to find, and remember—I knew Rusty Drake."

"Good point," Garcia said. "We'll see you later."

Connor cranked the engines and took off in the Widgeon minutes before the helicopter swept in to the airport, trailing the whistling sound of a turbine engine above the steady thump of the rotor blades, and landed near Rossi's police jeep.

"Agent Garcia, what is the FBI doing out here?" Lieutenant Wheeler said when he alighted from the helicopter. He was a tall, clean-cut man with a quick smile.

"Mister Dodge made some terroristic threats against the wind farm," Garcia said, "which is right in my wheelhouse."

"Fine, the more the merrier," Wheeler said. "We took a good look at Dodge's farm from the air and we didn't see any activity, so I say we go out and meet J.D. before the crime scene boys arrive."

"That works for me," Rossi said. "Let's get this over with."

Wheeler rode shotgun in Rossi's jeep while Garcia squeezed into the backseat with the two troopers. When they arrived at the pig farm, there was nobody in sight and J.D.'s tractor was parked alongside the barn.

"This isn't right," Rossi said when he stopped the jeep where the trail met the farm. "J.D. usually comes out to confront people when they get near his property."

"I agree," Garcia said. "By now J.D. is watching us, for sure."

Wheeler tilted his head toward his troopers and they pulled their assault rifles from the cases. Without a word they stood alongside the jeep and aimed the long guns toward the barn. They walked alongside on high alert when Rossi drove slowly to the side of the barn and stopped the jeep.

"It's my town," Rossi said when he dismounted. "So I guess I get to go first."

Then Rossi approached the barn with his .357 Magnum drawn and Garcia and Wheeler right behind him. One of the troopers stood cover near the jeep with his long gun while the other took a position alongside the door when Rossi made entry.

"Police," Rossi said, "we have a warrant. Show yourself, J.D., and keep your hands where we can see them."

"I don't think he can hear you," Garcia said when he shined his flashlight on a body sprawled across some bales of hay inside the barn. The congealed blood and brain matter and bone fragments around the head looked like a horrible stew in brown gravy that had been spilled on the hay.

"Don't step on this spent shell casing," Garcia said when Rossi and Wheeler came in for a look.

"If you ask me," Rossi said, "he knew we were coming to find Rusty's body, and eating a bullet was the only way out."

"That's on you, Rossi," Wheeler said. "You should have taken him into custody yesterday."

"It's a small island," Rossi said. "He had no place to hide."

Wheeler shrugged and Garcia said, "Is that his gun?"

"It looks like his pistol," Rossi said. "He carried it in his back pocket. What do you make of his pants being open?"

"Autoerotic suicide," Wheeler said. "Usually the victim hangs himself as he's getting off, but a gunshot isn't unheard of."

"Maybe he just wanted to hold on to his dick as long as he could," Garcia said, shining his flashlight to the side of J.D.'s corpse. "But I think we can rule out suicide—there's another spent shell casing over here."

"Two shots fired?" Rossi said. "Then maybe his pants are open because somebody shot his dick off after they killed him. There's a long list of people on this island who might hate him enough to do that."

"I'm not going to look to see if this stiff still has a wiener," Garcia said. "Are you?"

"No thanks," Wheeler said. "That's the medical examiner's job. Let's get out of here."

The Firepit

Lorraine and Betsy were driving away from the harbor after talking with Doctor Herman when Lorraine said, "Betsy, can I borrow the Woody after we get to your house?"

"Sure," Betsy said. "Where are you going?"

"Well, the boys are searching J.D.'s pig farm—and Logan is out on the *Racketeer*—so there is nobody home at his house."

"What are you going to do?" Betsy said. "Break into Logan's house?"

"Maybe," Lorraine said. "At the very least I want to snoop around outside and look in the windows."

"Great idea," Betsy said. "I'll go with you. Fact is, I don't feel like sitting at home while everybody else is doing something productive."

"That's the spirit," Lorraine said, and then Betsy turned away from the road to her own home and went down Center Road toward the south side of the island.

"There's no turning back now," Betsy said when she aimed the Woody up the narrow dirt path to the house, with no place to turn around until they reached the clearing on the bluffs.

Betsy parked the Woody a short distance away from the house, and the two women walked around to the deck on the back side—which was all floor-to-ceiling glass facing the ocean—and peered inside. There were discarded clothes and empty potato chip bags on the floor and the telescope on a tripod—which stood close to the windows—was aimed toward J.D.'s farm.

"We know one thing now," Betsy said, looking at spattered pots and pans and dirty dishes overflowing from the kitchen sink. "Logan is a real slob."

"Aren't all men?" Lorraine said.

"No," Betsy said. "Russell was actually a neat freak. It was one aspect of his minimalist lifestyle that I truly appreciated."

"Yes, but Rusty was one of a kind," Lorraine said. "You should try keeping a house with two sons and a fly-boy husband with his head in the clouds."

"I'm sure that keeps you on your toes," Betsy said.

"By the way," Lorraine said. "I'm sorry I didn't call to let you know I wouldn't be coming back to your house last night. I—"

"No need to explain," Betsy said. "No need at all."

"I just want you to know that I'm not usually that way. There was some unfinished business to take care of—but it's all over now—it's done."

"Of course," Betsy said. "I'm the last person who should make judgments, so I'm happy you worked it all out."

Lorraine said, "Thank you." Then, after a thoughtful pause she said, "Now, standing here you can see that Logan has a nearly perfect view of the south side of the island with his telescope. But when I was here on Sunday, it was pointed the other way, toward Rodmans Hollow."

"You mean he could see where Russell parked the Woody to go surfing?"

"Absolutely," Lorraine said. "What's more important is that Logan could have seen something falling out of the bluffs as the clay eroded. And the boys found tractor tracks leading to a stone wall that had been excavated."

"Now look here," Lorraine said, moving to the back of the deck and pointing to the grass. "What do you suppose made these tracks leading up to Logan's basement?"

"Those are tractor tracks," Betsy said.

"Exactly," Lorraine said. "It certainly looks like Logan saw something on the bluffs—something that had been buried for a long time. And I'm reasonably sure that he recruited J.D. to use his tractor to bring the treasure here."

Betsy said, "Did this treasure come from the U-853?"

"I don't know," Lorraine said. "Let's do some snooping."

Lorraine led her down to a bulkhead door to the basement, which was unlocked. The doors creaked when she opened them but they allowed enough sunlight into the basement that the women could see all four walls and a dusty concrete floor.

"There's nothing here," Betsy said. "This basement is completely empty."

"Yes," Lorraine said. "But look at these footprints in the dust on the floor. Someone dragged some heavy items to this door. So we'd better not disturb that bit of evidence."

They went back up the stairs to ground level and Lorraine closed the bulkhead door. Then they walked around the grass behind the house.

"What are we looking for?" Betsy said.

"I don't know," Lorraine said. "Maybe somebody dropped a clue."

There was a stone firepit behind the house and Lorraine picked a partially burned branch to stir the ashes, until she said, "What's this?"

"It looks like a hinge," Betsy said.

"It sure is a hinge," Lorraine said. "And here's more hardware—a clasp and screws. And look at this!"

"Oh my God," Betsy said when Lorraine held up a small piece of charred wood embossed with an eagle and a swastika.

"Here it is," Lorraine said. "Proof that Logan found Nazi gold on Block Island."

"Yes," Betsy said. "But how in the world could he have known where to look?"

"He didn't know," Lorraine said. "Logan is imbecilic—but he is lucky and crafty. If a normal person had sighted the treasure eroding out of the bluffs, they would have turned it over to the authorities for a handsome reward and fifteen minutes of fame. But not Logan. He immediately saw an opportunity to pay off the investors from his other schemes while keeping most of the gold for himself. The boys think he's putting some of the gold back onto the U-853, and now we can prove it."

"Oh," Betsy said, suddenly unsteady on her feet. Lorraine held her for a moment until she regained her equilibrium. Then she looked out to sea and said, "So it was just a cosmic coincidence that cost Russell his life—when he saw what Logan and J.D. were up to."

"I wouldn't call it a coincidence," Lorraine said. "Rusty spent so much time on the water that he was bound to see any mischief along this coast. And he was the one man who could immediately make the connection to the Tightrope Walker and the U-853. There's little doubt that he would have confronted J.D. and Logan to demand that they surrender their discovery so that it could be justly distributed."

"So," Betsy said, "what do we do now?"

"Now we take this evidence to Rene," Lorraine said. "I can't wait to show him what we've found."

"I hate to tell you this," Betsy said. "But your business from last night may not be as settled as you may think—your whole face just lit up when you mentioned Rene."

Then they both looked up when they heard the sound of a twin engine airplane flying low along the coast. When the unmistakable profile of a seaplane came into view and flew past them Betsy said, "Was that Connor?"

"Yes," Lorraine said. "He's making his approach to land at the airport. We should pick him up in a few minutes."

"Do you think he saw us here?"

"Connor sees everything," Lorraine said, as they walked back to the Woody. "He always has."

Fools' Courage

Lorraine and Connor were with Betsy that evening when Rossi came to the door, grim-faced. Connor let him into the house and then went outside to talk to Garcia, who was standing alongside the police jeep when he said, "I wouldn't want to be in Rossi's shoes right now."

"They found Rusty?"

"Yup," Garcia said. "In the mud under the pigsty. It wasn't pretty."

Connor said, "How—?"

"Looks like he was shot several times—once in the head."

"Damn it," Connor said. "He didn't deserve to go that way. Poor Betsy—this will be devastating."

When Rossi came out of the house a few minutes later, he said, "I need a drink. No—I need to get blotto."

"I'll second that," Garcia said.

The three men turned to look at Lorraine when she came out of the house after Rossi and said, "At least now Betsy knows."

"Right," Connor said. "Still—it's a rotten deal."

"It's awful," Lorraine said as she handed the charred piece of wood with the swastika to Garcia. "But I found this in Logan's firepit today. It looks like he burned some sort of Nazi storage box or shipping crate."

"Damn it," Garcia said. "This would have been good evidence."

"Would have been?" Lorraine said.

"The chain of custody is fractured," Garcia said. "There's no way I can prove that this came from Logan's firepit, much less that he put it there. A law school dropout could get this excluded from evidence at a trial."

"I'll put it back in the firepit so you can find it there yourself," Lorraine said.

"That could get tricky if I'm under oath in a courtroom," Garcia said. "But I'll take a close look at that firepit for other evidence."

"It's still a good clue," Connor said. "Even if it won't stand up in court, now we know that Logan already has something valuable from the U-853. And I can tell you one thing for sure—this wood hasn't been in salt water for sixty years."

"Isn't it obvious?" Rossi said. "That wood was in the dry clay on the bluff in Rodmans Hollow—where the Tightrope Walker buried it in 1945—and the tire tracks at Logan's house came from J.D.'s tractor. That's all I need to arrest Logan right now."

"That would be the safe thing to do," Garcia said. "But maybe we should try for a grand slam. Now we know that Logan found the Nazi treasure on dry land, so he has to be secretly putting it on the U-853. His divers must have been hiding the treasure deep within the wreck to make it look like a new discovery."

"That's right," Connor said. "I'm betting that they've been stashing gold deep under that torpedo we saw on our night dive. Nobody else has been dumb enough to tamper with that warhead, but they were willing to take the risk—it's a case of fools' courage."

"Okay, I'll ask the question," Lorraine said. "Why go to all the trouble of putting gold on a shipwreck?"

"He's putting on a show," Garcia said. "The U-853 is just a diversion. Logan knows that he won't get to keep any of that gold, because there will be one hell of a court battle over any treasure from the U-853. The Germans will want it back, and so will half the countries in Europe that were plundered in the war."

"Not to mention the Holocaust victims and their families," Connor said. "After all—and I'm sorry but this isn't a pleasant thought—a lot of Nazi gold came from the jewelry and household items of Jews—and the fillings from their teeth."

"Oh my God," Lorraine said.

"This is dirty business all around," Rossi said. "So how do we wrap it up?"

"Didn't you say that tomorrow is the last day of Logan's charter of the *Racketeer*?" Garcia said. "That means he'll have to bring the treasure up soon, so we have to be ready to move in on him."

"I think you're right about that," Connor said. "Of course, I'm betting that Logan put some of the treasure aside for himself, so he can ride off into the sunset while his investors fight the court battle for what was brought up from the U-853."

"Now I get it," Rossi said. "Dirk and Honey left the island with the rest of the gold. So you want to let Logan lead us to them when he goes to collect his loot."

"I don't know about that," Lorraine said. "I don't think those love-birds need Logan at all. If they have any gold, they're long gone by now."

"We have ways to find them," Garcia said. "The main thing is we need to let Logan bring up the treasure and think that everything is going according to his plan. That's how we catch him in the act."

"In that case," Connor said, "I'll go out on the *Racketeer* as Tony's deckhand tomorrow."

"We should both go," Garcia said.

"I don't think so," Connor said. "They've seen you with Rossi so they've made you as a cop already, but I'm just an old friend of Captain Tony's from Newport."

"Connor is right," Rossi said. "He's the only one of us who could act like a real deckhand on a boat. But it will be risky, so I'll commandeer one of the island fishing boats to take me out and hang out nearby like they're just trawling their nets. That way I'll be close enough to help if the plan goes south."

"That's a great idea," Connor said.

"Connor, are you crazy?" Lorraine said. "You can't take a chance like that. These people already committed two murders—what makes you think it can't happen to you?"

"Don't worry," Connor said. "This is going to be a cakewalk. I'll be there as a witness when they bring up the gold, that's all. Garcia and Rossi can take care of business when the *Racketeer* gets back to the dock."

"You're impossible," Lorraine said as she turned and went back into the house.

When Lorraine was out of earshot Connor said, "She'll get over it."

"We're going into town to tie one on," Rossi said. "Are you in?"

"No thanks," Connor said. "I'm not much of a drinker anymore—I'll stay here tonight. Lorraine will give me a ride to the boat in the morning."

Saturday, May 14

Gold Rising

The moon was setting and the day was little more than a faint glow gathering above the water to the east when Lorraine brought Connor to Old Harbor, where Rossi was sitting in his jeep near the *Racketeer*.

"Connor, I don't like this," Rossi said. "You're going to be outnumbered on that boat, and it will take me a long time to get to you if there is trouble."

"Listen to him," Lorraine said. "This is crazy. It will be three against one if something goes wrong."

"Three against two," Connor said. "Tony will have my back—I like those odds."

"Were the hell is Rene?" Lorraine said. "I was counting on him to talk you out of this."

"Garcia said something about sleeping in this morning," Rossi said. "He didn't want to come on the *Betty Jane* with me because he had some other lead to follow up on."

"Listen, both of you," Connor said. "This is going to be a cakewalk. I'm only going because Tony needs help on deck today, and we need to see exactly what they bring to the surface."

"What are you going to do if they decide to make off with the loot?" Lorraine said. "Once they have the treasure onboard, they might force Tony to take them someplace else where they can stage a getaway. Have you thought about that?"

"I'll be ready if they try some funny business," Connor said, tapping the .45 hidden under his sweatshirt. "Now you two should get out of here—we don't want Logan and his boys to see you."

"Be careful," Lorraine said, when she gave Connor a hug and a kiss. Then before she got into the Woody, she said, "I'm going to wake up Rene."

"Keep that flare gun handy," Rossi said to Connor as he started the engine of his jeep. "I'll be a mile away on the *Betty Jane* watching for your signal."

When Connor stepped down from the dock onto the *Racketeer*, Tony was sitting in his chair at the helm with a cup of coffee.

"Connor," Tony said. "What the hell are you doing here?"

"I'm going to be your mate today," Connor said. "Is there more of that coffee in the pot?"

"I didn't ask for no mate today," Tony said.

"Of course you didn't," Connor said as he poured a cup for himself. "Because you're a stubborn old seadog who wouldn't ask for someone to throw you a life ring if you were drowning. So I'm coming anyway."

"Well, I guess that's okay," Tony said. "I'm not sure my legs will hold up today. This has been a tough charter, I'll tell you that much! Those sons-a-bitches haven't lifted a finger to help me with chores on the boat all week long. So, welcome aboard."

The sun was well above the horizon by the time Logan arrived in the Hummer with Rick and Brownie. He was carrying his professional video camera—and his mood was uncharacteristically buoyant when he said, "Today is the big day! You'll see! Soon everybody will be talking about this!"

"Talking about what?" Connor said.

"What are you doing here?" Logan said. "Aren't you the loser with the crappy old airplane?"

"Yeah, that's him," Brownie said, standing to the side.

"Tony needs a little help running the boat today," Connor said. "You've been running him ragged this week, so I'm coming aboard as his mate. Now, what's the big event?"

"You'll see what we bring up from the U-boat today," Logan said. "Everybody is going to be amazed. This island is going to be crawling with the news media in a few hours. I've already called all the networks to notify them about what we found on that submarine. You'll see!"

Connor helped Tony stow the scuba air bottles when Rick and Brownie handed them down to the boat. Then he took in the lines after Tony started the engines and soon the *Racketeer* was pointed out to sea, with the three treasure hunters sitting on the transom with their butts hanging over the stern, talking in whispers.

"I'm tempted to gun the engines and toss those bozos overboard," Tony said when Connor was standing next to him at the steering station. "Then we could pretend we didn't see them drowning."

"Except that you're a good captain," Connor said. "Nobody is going to drown on your boat."

"I suppose you're right," Tony said. By then the *Racketeer* was clear of the breakwater and gently heaving on long ocean swells coming in from offshore, and Logan's trio went into the cabin to lie down.

"Connor, why don't you take a trick at the wheel?" Tony said. "You know where we're going."

Connor pushed the helmsman's seat away when he took the wheel, and Tony said, "Yeah, I forgot—you like to stand when you drive a boat."

"At first I do," Connor said. "I like to feel the boat's motion under my feet, at least until I get to know how she handles the waves."

"That's good," Tony said. When he refilled his coffee cup, he added some to Connor's as well. Then he said, "You should really have a boat, Conner. Look astern of us at that wake you are making—it's perfectly straight. I couldn't do any better. You got salt water in your veins and I know the ocean is calling to you. Why don't you get another boat, Connor? A man shouldn't deny his urges—it ain't healthy."

"I'm thinking about it," Connor said.

"Get something with a high bow and twin diesel engines," Tony said. "Forget that useless sailboat crap, you need a boat you can do things with—fishing and diving and going where you want to go no matter what the damn wind is doing."

"Captain Tony, are you trying to sell me the *Racketeer*?"

"Hey, that's a good idea," Tony said. "That's a damn good idea."

"I'll have to think about that," Connor said.

Tony took the helm from Connor and slowed the engines when they approached the small anchoring buoy above the wreck, and Connor snagged the line with a boathook and made it fast to the cleat on the *Racketeer*'s bow.

"Thanks," Tony said, after the engines were shut down and the boat was riding swells on the anchor line. "I've been doing that by myself all week—steering the boat and cleating the lines—because this gang is too lazy to lift a finger."

When Logan's gang came up from the cabin—stretching and yawning after their nap—Logan filmed with the video camera while Rick and Brownie put on their gear. Then the two divers went into the water and descended along the anchor line carrying a plastic milk crate, with Connor holding the bitter end of the line, which would be used the raise the makeshift basket. The divers had only been on the bottom for a few minutes when Connor felt two jerks on the tending line and he began lifting hand over hand, dropping the excess line to the deck in neat coils.

"You should not have doubted me, old man," Logan said. "Now you're going to see how smart I really am—everybody is going to see that I really know what I'm doing."

Even before it broke the surface, Connor could see two gold bars glowing in the basket.

"I'll be damned," Connor said, when he placed the milk crate on the deck and picked up one of the bars, which was about seven inches long and weighed nearly thirty pounds. The smooth surface of the gold was lustrous but darker than Connor had expected, and it bore the inscription *Deutsche Reichsbank*. There was also a stylized eagle atop a swastika stamped into the precious metal—this was the *Reichsadler*, the Reich's Eagle—the hateful symbol of the Nazi Party.

"Do you believe me now?" Logan said. "That one piece of gold is worth more money than you ever had—or ever will have."

"This is insane," Connor said, realizing that Logan was filming him as he spoke. "How could gold have been missed on this wreck? Divers blasted the hull of the U-853 open years ago and probed every nook and cranny."

"I knew where to look," Logan said. "I knew to look where nobody else dared to go. I'm the only person on Earth who could do this. Now lower that crate down again—there's more where these two came from."

Connor was lowering the basket for another load when Tony came onto the aft deck and saw the two gold bars that Connor had just hauled up.

"This isn't right," Tony said. "This is too easy."

"Relax, Captain," Connor said. "Let's just get this gold aboard and we can sort it all out later."

"No," Tony said. "I don't want this on my boat. It's not a square deal, Connor. This is all wrong, and nobody will believe that I wasn't in on this all the way."

"Trust me," Connor said. "This will all work out. Let's get the gold aboard and recover the divers and then we can sort it out when we get back to the island."

By the time Tony sat down, the crate was on the bottom and Connor felt another two tugs on the tending line.

"You don't seem very eager to touch your treasure," Connor said, as Logan kept filming every move. "Don't you want to hold one of these gold bars in your hands?"

"Just bring that basket up again," Logan said.

"That seems odd," Connor said, hauling the line hand over hand. "After years of searching you find your treasure—and you don't have the urge to touch it? Could it be that you have fondled these bars before?"

"You're talking trash, old man. I figured this out, I knew where to look. Nobody else had the balls to look under that torpedo."

"This metal doesn't look like it has been under seawater for sixty years," Connor said when he hauled the crate up to the deck again, with another two gold bars.

"That's because of the way it was protected," Logan said. "Besides, gold doesn't rust or corrode, ever."

"Logan—you're an imbecile," Connor said, looking directly into the camera lens. "I know that this gold came out of the bluffs at Rodmans Hollow. You saw it with the telescope in your living room the morning after the cliff eroded enough to expose it, didn't you?"

"Shut up!" Logan said. "You're ruining this video. Just shut up!"

"Is this why you killed Rusty Drake?" Connor said, holding a gold bar up to the camera. "Rusty saw you and J.D. Dodge at Rodmans Hollow when he was surfing, isn't that right? When he followed you and J.D. taking the gold away in the tractor, you murdered him to protect your secret. Then J.D. drove Rusty's Woody back to Rodmans Hollow and tossed his surfboard in the water to make it look like a drowning."

"I didn't murder anybody," Logan said, lowering the camera and his gaze, unable to look at Connor's eyes. "That was all J.D."

"Good," Connor said. "So you admit it—you and your boys didn't find this gold on the U-853—you put it down there."

"Why would I do a dumb thing like that?"

"Because you couldn't claim treasure you found on a nature preserve, or in the backyard of the house you were renting since the landowners would have laid claim to any gold found on their property. So you had the idea to stash it back on the U-853 so you could claim maritime salvage rights, as if it never came ashore."

"That's bullshit!" Logan said.

"I have to admit—you were crafty," Connor said as he lowered the basket again. "You knew that you'd have to explain where the gold came from—you couldn't just put this amount on the market with no documents to show where it originated."

"I was more than crafty," Logan said. "I was a genius."

"Maybe you were," Connor said, as he leaned over the side to haul the basket up again. "After all, you solved the problem with your investors, too. They thought you were looking for a missing atom bomb in Savannah—but they'll be satisfied with gold from a U-boat, won't they?"

"They'll get their money back," Logan said. "And then some."

"Maybe," Connor said when he laid two more gold bars on the deck and then sent the basket down again. "Of course, they'll be fighting court battles with the German government and half the people in Europe for years over who should get the gold—personally, I vote for the families of Holocaust victims and survivors to get it all—but that won't bother you too much. Because you didn't place all the gold on the U-boat, did you, Logan? Didn't you leave some of it aside for yourself?"

"I see," Logan said, exhaling heavily and crossing his arms on his chest. "I may have underestimated you, old man. How much of a cut do you want?"

"My cut?" Connor said. "My cut is going to be a big problem for you, Logan. Because all I want is justice for our friend Rusty. So tough break, buddy—you're going to prison for two murders—and I hope you live a long life behind bars. That will be my cut."

"What is that—two murders? What are you saying?"

"Somebody killed J.D.," Connor said as he hauled the basket up and put the seventh and eighth gold bars on the deck. "It had to be you. After all, you don't like to share."

"They can't pin that on me," Logan said. "I didn't kill anybody. In fact, I don't even know J.D. Dodge—I never even met him, and you can't prove otherwise. You're just making up a big conspiracy theory. None of that stuff happened—we found this gold on the submarine, that's all there is to it—so it's your word against mine."

"Your word is worthless, Logan. You're a knucklehead—a crafty one—but still a knucklehead. You can't talk your way out of this."

"Maybe you're right," Logan said, when he turned and reached into his pocket and pulled out a compact Colt Defender pistol—small, but deadly at close range. "Maybe you're about to fall overboard and drown. But first you need to send that basket down—there are two more gold bars waiting to come up."

"Big mistake," Connor said as Tony stood up behind Logan and instantly landed a fist at the base of his skull. Connor swiped the pistol out of Logan's hand in the same moment that he stumbled to his knees from the unexpected force of the old boxer's punch.

"No guns," Tony said. "Nobody likes a punk with a gun."

Then Connor and Tony both turned when a voice from inside the boat said, "That's enough, gentlemen."

Stakeout

"Where the hell did you come from?" Connor said when Garcia came up the stairway from the *Racketeer*'s cabin with a pistol in his hand.

"I came in through the bow hatch while Tony was sleeping in the pilothouse and stowed away as far forward as I could last night," Garcia said. "*Racketeer*'s forepeak compartment is a bit cramped, but I've been on worse stakeouts."

"Right," Connor said. "You could have come up a little sooner—this punk almost took a shot at me."

"I had Logan covered the whole time," Garcia said as he holstered his pistol. "Except that Tony stepped in the way to slug him just before I was going to shoot him."

Then he produced a pair of silver handcuffs and slapped them on Logan's wrists as he said, "You're under arrest."

"For what?" Logan said. "I didn't do anything."

"You just implicated yourself in conspiracy to commit fraud, theft, and murder," Garcia said. "I was listening to every word you said to Connor, especially the part where you said there were two more gold bars down in the wreck."

"Exactly," Connor said. "How would you know how much gold was in the U-boat—unless you put it there?"

"Miranda! You can't use that," Logan said, nearly wailing. "I wasn't advised of my rights. Miranda!"

"Those statements were spontaneous declarations," Garcia said as he sat down and pulled off his cowboy boots. "Miranda only applies if I question you. Since Connor didn't know that I was listening, every word you said is admissible."

"What the hell are you doing?" Connor said as Garcia also pulled his dungarees off.

"I'm going diving," Garcia said as he selected some of the spare scuba gear from Tony's collection. "Send that basket back down—and grab that dry suit I used the other night out of the cabin, will you? It's under the bunk on the starboard side."

"You can't go down there alone," Connor said as he lowered the basket. "I'll suit up, too."

"Then who will watch Logan?" Garcia said. "I have to do this alone. It will be a spike dive—down and up—with no bottom time and no need to decompress. If I see where these guys stashed the gold on the wreck, we'll have a good case against them—and if I see them in the act of removing gold from their hiding spot, it will be an airtight indictment."

"You don't have to go alone," Connor said. "Rossi isn't far away on another boat. Let me signal him to come here."

"There's no time for that," Garcia said. "I have to catch them in the act—which means right now."

Tony handed Garcia a dry suit and he quickly donned the rest of his equipment. When he was sitting on the gunwale ready to go into the water, he looked at Connor and said, "Connor, I—Lorraine—"

"What?" Connor said.

"I—want you to turn Logan over to Rossi as soon as you can."

"Turn him over yourself," Connor said.

"Right," Garcia said, just before he put the regulator in his mouth and did a backflip off the rail. "Just in case."

As soon as Garcia disappeared down the anchor line trailing bubbles, Connor went to the steering station and fired the flare gun.

"You son of a bitch!" Tony said, standing above Logan on the aft deck. "You got me into this mess! You lied to me! I told you I didn't want any part of a crime—nothing—not even jaywalking! Remember?"

"Yell at him all you want," Connor said, when the old boxer raised a fist in anger. "But you can't hit him, Tony."

"Damn it all to hell!" Tony said as he became more agitated. "This isn't right! Nobody is going to count me as innocent—they never do. I'm just an old mobster—they don't even ask for my side of the story."

"Take it easy," Connor said. "Garcia and Rossi both know the score—they won't let you take the rap for any part in this."

"This damn gold!" Tony said as he picked a bar off the deck and held it up. "This stuff drives men crazy! I don't want it on my boat!"

"Tony, don't!" Connor said. But it was too late—Tony hurled the gold bar over the side of the boat and it splashed into the dark water. Then he reached down and took another bar of gold in his hand and pitched it over the side of the *Racketeer*—followed by two more gold bars together, one in each hand—before Connor could stop him.

Seventeen fathoms under the Racketeer, *Garcia saw Rick and Brownie near the new hole in the bow of the U-853 that Connor had explored on their night dive. As he descended, he saw they had dragged the torpedo's warhead out of the hull to get to a space behind where it had been entombed in the innards of the wreck for six decades. The two were hovering over a few gold bars on the bottom when something shot past Garcia's head like a golden comet with a tail of silver bubbles and hit the bottom hard near them. Then another something flashed by—gold! Garcia suddenly realized—he grabbed for the fourth bar as it shot past him, even though he knew it was futile and that he would not be able to stop its inevitable trajectory toward the torpedo warhead. The gold closed in on the high explosive as if guided by some unseen hand—Garcia thought of his children and his mother and his ex-wife—but in the last instant of his life he thought—Lorraine—*

The explosion erupted up through the water like an undersea volcano, releasing a geyser of energy under the *Racketeer* that swelled up from the depths and wrenched the boat's hull in half. Connor felt himself flying backward through the air—his world was a blur within a roar—and he wasn't certain which way was up when he landed in the water.

Debris from the *Racketeer* was landing in the water around Connor—the helmsman's chair and a hatch cover and seat cushions and a cooler full of ice—and then he saw Tony treading water nearby and he swam to him.

"Tony, are you hurt?" Connor said, spitting saltwater with his words.

"Yeah, I'm okay—I think."

"Where's Logan?"

"I'm holding him," Tony said. "Help me get his head above water."

"I'm not sure I want to save him," Connor said, when he realized that Tony was trying to pull the handcuffed man to the surface.

"I can't let this asshole drown," Tony said. "Like it or not, he's a passenger on the *Racketeer*."

"You're right, Captain," Connor said as he reached down to tug Logan's head above the surface.

Logan was screaming and crying and vomiting when the trawler *Betty Jane* pulled up alongside the three survivors. Rossi reached down to grasp Logan by the scruff, hauling him out of the water and dropping him on the deck like a netted fish before he helped Tony and Connor onto the boat.

"What about Rick and Brownie?"

"They're done for," Connor said. "They were on the bottom when the torpedo exploded."

"A torpedo?" Rossi said.

"It had to be that torpedo warhead Garcia and I saw the other night," Connor said.

"Speaking of Garcia," Rossi said, "we can't find him anywhere on the island."

"He was a stowaway," Tony said. "I can't believe I didn't spot him before we left the dock. I guess I was just too tired or something."

"He was on the *Racketeer*?" Rossi said.

"Right," Connor said. "Then he suited up and went down to catch those knuckleheads in the act—"

"You mean he was in the water for that explosion?"

"I couldn't stop him," Connor said. "Nobody could."

The Circle

Lorraine and Betsy were sitting in Ballard's waiting for Connor and Rossi to return when they heard the explosion and ran outside to try to see what had happened. But there was no sign of the *Racketeer*. They stood on the beach with their hearts in their throats until a fisherman came to them saying that he had heard a ship-to-shore radio transmission from the *Betty Jane* stating that they had picked up survivors and that Rossi, Connor, and Tony were okay.

A small crowd had gathered at the dock and the *Betty Jane* was in sight and not far from Old Harbor when a news helicopter landed on the beach and discharged a reporter and a cameraman. The TV reporter saw Lorraine's notebook and recognized her as a journalist, so he walked straight to her and said, "What's going on?"

"We don't know yet," Lorraine said.

"How did you get the scoop on this?" the television reporter said. "We got a call this morning saying that some fabulous discovery had been made on the U-boat—something that everybody else had missed. But there was no mention of an explosion."

"I'm not after a story," Lorraine said, pointing to the *Betty Jane*. "My husband is on that boat. And by the way, your source only gave you one version of events, so I'd hold off with the headline on your report until you have a little more information."

"Sure, but the explosion was heard—and felt—as far away as Westerly and North Kingston," the TV man said. "So we have to tell the newsroom something right now."

"Try telling them that there is no immediate danger to the public," Lorraine said. "And that the story is still developing."

A high-speed Coast Guard boat escorted the *Betty Jane* into Old Harbor, and the island rescue squad arrived on the dock in front of Ballard's. Lorraine could see Connor and Rossi standing on the deck as the boat tied up.

"Get out of the way," Connor said, with his jaw set as he stepped off the *Betty Jane* and pushed past the cameras and the onlookers to help Tony to the rescue squad, while Rossi dragged Logan off the boat.

"Brian," Betsy said to Rossi, "are you okay?"

"I'm fine," Rossi said. Then he pushed Logan to the EMTs and said, "Check this gentleman out before I lock him up."

After Connor sat Tony in the rescue vehicle Lorraine said, "What happened?"

"The *Racketeer* got blown out of the water," Connor said.

"My boat is gone," Tony said. "How will I earn a living without her?"

"I can't find Rene anywhere on the island," Lorraine said.

"Garcia was a stowaway on the *Racketeer* today," Connor said. "He was diving down to the wreck to catch those guys in the act when the torpedo exploded. The Coast Guard will keep searching, but—"

"No—" Lorraine said, gasping. "Is there any hope?"

"Not a chance, Peaches—but I'm okay."

"Thank God for that," Lorraine said. But as she hugged her husband she was also looking over his shoulder, out to sea, and her eyes became teary.

The group hardly noticed when the *Metacomet* arrived from Point Judith and backed into the ferry slip, but there was a scrum of reporters and cameramen aboard, and they streamed off the boat to quickly surround the rescue squad.

"Can you tell our viewers what happened out there?" ... "Was that a torpedo?" ... "How much gold did you find?" ... "Where is the treasure now? Can we see it?"

Unbeknownst to their parents, Bennett and Natalie also arrived on the *Metacomet*, and they pushed through the crowd to get next to Connor, where Bennett said, "Dad, are you okay?"

"I'm fine, Ben. But what are you two doing out here?"

"Our surfboards are still in Rusty's shed," Bennett said. "We came out to get them, and to see Miss Betsy. So what happened?"

"You picked a really bad time to show up," Lorraine said as she turned to the teenagers. "We'll explain all this later."

"Where is Mr. Garcia?" Bennett said. "Isn't he helping you here on the island?"

"He was," Lorraine said. "But there's been an accident."

"You mean that big explosion we heard?"

"I'm afraid so," Connor said, talking over Lorraine's shoulder.

Natalie said, "Is he—?"

"I'm afraid we've lost Mister Garcia," Connor said.

"That sucks," Bennett said, as he put his arm around Natalie and turned away.

A reporter shoved a microphone in Connor's face and said, "What boat were you on?"

"The *Racketeer*," Connor said. "Out of Newport, Rhode Island."

"Isn't that Tony Marino's boat?" another reporter said. "Isn't he connected to the Mob on Federal Hill?"

"He's sitting right there," Connor said, nodding to Tony. "So you better be careful not to call Captain Tony a gangster—because if he doesn't stand up and slug you, I will."

"Gimme a break, fellas," Tony said. "My boat is gone—how am I going to earn a living now?"

The scrum of reporters and tourists with cameras tightened around them until several commercial fishermen in rubber boots and the cook from Ballard's in a white apron came over and pushed the onlookers away. Connor was still wet so an EMT draped a blanket over his shoulders.

"You should sit down," the EMT said. "If you're not going into shock, you should be."

"Right," Connor said, staying on his feet. "Thanks, buddy, but I'm okay."

The island residents who were holding the reporters and tourists at bay allowed town manager Tom Champlin and *Block Island Times* editor Leif Carlson past their lines, and Carlson said, "Is everybody okay?"

"No," Rossi said. "Two divers got blown to hell. And it looks like we lost an FBI agent who was working on the case."

"What's this about gold on the U-boat?" Champlin said. "There's a rumor going around that the gold was first found on the bluffs near Rodmans Hollow, which means it all belongs to the town."

"Sorry to disappoint you," Connor said. "But the underwater explosion that sank the *Racketeer* probably vaporized every gold bar within ten feet of that torpedo warhead. Divers will be finding gold nuggets all around the U-853 for decades—so good luck claiming that for the town."

Rossi said, "Where did you hear that rumor about the gold and Rodmans Hollow, Tom?"

"I don't know," Champlin said. "I guess it was from Miss Hattie."

"There's nothing surprising about that," Lorraine said. "All rumors on this island seem to point to Hattie."

"If you'll excuse me," Rossi said, pulling Logan to his feet. "Right now I have to toss this suspect into a cell at my office."

"I didn't do anything illegal," Logan said, suddenly finding his voice. "My business is totally legitimate. You'll see! When a jury sees all the evidence, I'll be free and clear. You'll see!"

"What are the charges?" Champlin said.

"We'll start with conspiracy to defraud the government of the United States," Rossi said. "And two counts of first-degree murder."

"What?" Logan said. "I never killed nobody!"

"You better get yourself a good lawyer," Connor said. "Because you all but admitted to killing Rusty Drake when he confronted you about the gold."

"That wasn't me!" Logan said. "J.D. did that all on his own. I had nothing to do with that. That was just me talking trash, man."

"You bastard," Betsy said. "How could you kill a man over gold that didn't belong to you in the first place? I hope you rot in prison."

"I hate you," Bennett said, standing between Connor and Lorraine.

"You don't mean that," Natalie said, pulling Bennett back after the words were spoken.

"I'm telling you," Logan said. "I didn't do that. It wasn't me."

"Maybe not," Connor said. "But you were an accomplice, and then you killed J.D. to cover your tracks and make off with the gold, including his share. Isn't that right?"

"No!" Logan said.

Then a rotund little man stepped out through a ripple in the wall of locals holding back the curious crowd. "Excuse me," he said, "but I believe you are overlooking one important fact."

"Who are you?" Champlin said.

"This is Doctor Louis Herman from Milwaukee," Lorraine said. "And he has some interesting theories about this whole affair."

"Quite so," the doctor said. "You may find that J.D. was killed by someone else. Someone who knew—who had always known—that there was a great deal of gold hidden somewhere on this island."

"Who would that be?" Rossi said.

The doctor looked at Lorraine and said, "Would you care to elucidate my theory, Miss Lorraine?"

"Doctor Herman believes that only someone with Nazi tendencies would know that the gold was hidden on the island," Lorraine said. "Someone whose family operated the guest house that was intended to be the Tightrope Walker's sanctuary the night he came ashore—someone named Wagner."

There was a minor commotion in the crowd when the fishermen pulled Hattie to the front and thrust her into the circle of friends, where she blinked and cowered in the sunlight and the gaze of the crowd.

"Hattie Wagner?" Rossi said.

"Leave me alone," Hattie said. Her clothing was even more disheveled than usual, and her glasses were doubly crooked on her nose. "You all know me—just leave me alone, I say."

"Hattie," Lorraine said. "You have some explaining to do."

"Wait a minute," Champlin said. "We should take this conversation to the privacy of my office."

"I don't think so," Rossi said. "Not your office, and not behind closed doors at the police station. There have been too many secrets on this island, so you can fire me tomorrow but today we're doing this my way."

Then Rossi turned to Hattie and said, "I'm not going to ask you any questions and I'll advise you of your rights before you make a formal statement. But if you want to refute these allegations that have been made in public, this is your chance."

"Look at me," Hattie said. "I'm a small woman. How could I hurt a nasty old polecat like J.D.?"

"You did it easily," Lorraine said. "Because you had J.D. at a disadvantage when you lured him onto the hay in the barn and pulled his pants down."

"Watch what you say!" Hattie said. "Don't go starting no rumors against my reputation."

"Actually, your reputation is well known but seldom mentioned," Lorraine said. "You were quite popular with the boys on this island back in the day, weren't you, Hattie? Especially the Dodge boys. So when you took J.D. the barn to do some sparking—just for old times' sake—he was happy to have you on top of him."

"He was going to leave the island!" Hattie said. "I knew he had a fast boat stashed in New Harbor. I knew that J.D. stole the gold and he was going get away. I had to stop him."

"Right," Lorraine said. "So you unbuttoned his pants and entertained him until you could grab his pistol out of his back pocket—then you shot him."

"No!" Hattie said. "That's not what happened. It was self-defense."

"Oh?" Loraine said. "The only thing I wonder about is why you fired two shots."

"He was laughing at me," Hattie said. "I had his pistol and he wouldn't tell me where the gold was. He wouldn't even share! He was laughing and telling me to finish what I started in his pants. I couldn't let him steal my family's gold, could I?"

Lorraine said, "Then what happened?"

"He tried to get the pistol away from me. He was going to shoot me, I tell you. It went off when he tried to grab it and then when he was yelling at me his big mouth was wide open—and I just pushed the gun in there to scare him but it went off and made a big mess out of J.D.'s head and I just ran out of there. What else could I do?"

"Hold on just a minute," Connor said. "What makes you think that Nazi gold belongs to your family?"

"Because we took the big risk and kept the secrets for years," Hattie said. "My mother had a shortwave radio in the attic and she used to listen every night at a certain time—to this day I won't say exactly when—and the U-boats would transmit their messages, so short that nobody could get a line on them. We searched for the gold around Dorie's Cove for years without knowing that the Coast Guard was lying about that night."

"Hattie," Connor said, "who was the Tightrope Walker?"

"He was a great man," Hattie said. "If only he didn't get shot! Sebastian would have changed everything."

"So it was Sebastian Klaus," Connor said. "You know what this means? They're going to have to revise the history books to show that Joseph Goebbels's propaganda secretary actually made it to our shores."

"Yes," Hattie said. "I wasn't born yet when he spent summers at our guest house when his family lived in America, but I sure knew who he was. My mother—God rest her soul—told us all about what a great man he was and how he would change the world forever."

"Exactly how would he do that?" Lorraine said.

"He would work behind the scenes, of course," Hattie said. "But he would know how to use that gold to start a new movement in America—the

White Nationalist Workers' Party will change everything. Just wait until the steelworkers and plumbers and factory workers take over the government—wait until they rally around a strong man—then we'll get some things done!"

"Right," Rossi said, taking Hattie by the arm. "That's enough, Miss Wagner. You're under arrest."

"Don't you understand?" Hattie said, yelling over her shoulder as Rossi handcuffed her in his jeep. "We need a strong man who can get things done. We all have to unite behind one leader whose word is law because all this arguing makes the world a dangerous place. We need a leader who will drive the blacks and the Mexicans out of our country—and the Jews. Most of all we have to get rid of the Jews to have a pure white country. That's what America was in the beginning and that is how it should always be, a white country for good people only. We are the real patriots—God bless America!"

"I can't believe this is happening," Betsy said.

"We have to face it head-on," Lorraine said. "Most of all we have to consider the sort of country we might have today if Klaus had succeeded in igniting a powerful white nationalist movement here—fueled by Nazi rhetoric and Nazi gold."

The sound of the whistle above the *Metacomet*'s wheelhouse interrupted the group with a short blast signaling one minute until departure.

"Dad," Bennett said, "can we fly home with you?"

"Of course you can," Connor said. "We're leaving soon."

"Can we bring our surfboards on the airplane?" Natalie said.

"Sure," Connor said. "We can get them out of Rusty's shed when Miss Betsy gives us a ride to the airport. We should be able to shoehorn them into the Widgeon."

Then Connor turned to Tony and said, "You might as well come with us, Captain. There's nothing more to be done here."

"I guess you're right," Tony said. "The *Racketeer* was all I had on this island."

"Right," Lorraine said. "But I think I'll stay on the island one more night. I don't want to leave Betsy alone at a time like this."

"She won't be alone," Rossi said. "I'll come over to your house as soon as the state police take these two suspects from my jail cell. If that's okay, Betsy?"

"That would be fine, Brian. Please come tonight."

"You know," Connor said, as he walked to the Woody with his arm around Lorraine. "It's been a hell of a week, but at least it seems to be ending on a good note."

Epilogue

Betsy took them to the airport, and Connor sat Lorraine in the copilot's seat. His preflight inspection was completed and he was ready to start the Widgeon's engines as soon as the teenagers got the surfboards into the cabin and climbed in themselves.

"Is the boarding ladder aboard?" Connor said, over his shoulder. "And is the hatch closed and locked?"

"Roger that," Bennett said, strapping himself into the rear-facing seat behind his father. "We're all set back here."

"Good," Connor said. "Let's go." Then he yelled "Clear!" out the window and started the engines. Tony had taken the rearmost seat in the cabin and he declined a headset, but the teenagers were plugged into the intercom system so they could hear conversations over the noise of the engines.

Connor taxied to the runway and ran up the engines to be certain that they were operating properly before he released the brakes and pushed the throttles all the way forward and the Widgeon ambled down the runway before lifting off. The takeoff was to the west so Connor circled low around the south side of the island and then turned north around the Southeast Lighthouse and flew up the east side of the island, past Old Harbor and the town of New Shoreham. The ferry *Metacomet* was past North Reef and halfway across to Point Judith by then, and Connor eased the nose of the Widgeon down to make a gentle descent and a low pass alongside the ferry.

"That funny little doctor didn't waste any time leaving the island," Connor said when he saw the rotund form of a man standing on the stern of the boat, alongside a sidecar motorcycle and a tall figure clad in black leather.

Herman watched the Widgeon sweep in toward the *Metacomet* and he actually waved as Connor flew by not much higher than the vessel's mast. But the driver in black leathers never looked up from a comic book.

"That motorcycle driver gives me the creeps," Bennett said, pressing his face to the window alongside his seat. "Did you see how close he—I mean she—was standing next to me on the dock at Ballard's when you were ripping Hattie and Logan a new ass?"

"Bennett," Lorraine said. "Watch your language, please."

"I only hope we don't see them when the ferry pulls into Point Judith," Natalie said.

"We're going to get there before the ferry even comes through the breakwater at the Harbor of Refuge," Connor said. "That will give you two plenty of time to paddle ashore and get to Ben's jeep. So just come straight home and you probably will never see that pair again."

"What about Honey and Dirk?" Natalie said. "Will we ever see them again?"

"Forget about them," Connor said. "They're not your concern."

"That's right," Lorraine said. "They're probably lounging on some tropical beach right now, but the law will catch up with them eventually."

When they reached Point Judith, Connor descended over the lighthouse and the cottages at Sand Hill Cove and splashed down in the relatively calm water behind the breakwaters of the Harbor of Refuge. The Widgeon touched the ripples on the surface gently, but even so, geysers of spray cascaded over the entire airplane as the hull settled into the water.

"Wow," Lorraine said. "Does that happen every time?"

"Yes," Connor said. "Even the best water landing in this airplane looks like a crash. It's a big airframe to set down on the water."

Conner took the Widgeon close to the beach and cut the engines, where Natalie jumped out into waist-deep water. Bennett passed their surfboards out before he also jumped into the water and then the teens waved good-bye and paddled toward the beach.

"Do you want me to get off here?" Tony said, when Connor went back to the cabin to secure the hatch.

"Why?" Connor said. "Don't you want to fly to Newport with us? It's only a ten-minute flight from here."

"Let's just say that airplanes aren't my favorite way of traveling," Tony said. "That landing on the water was one hell of an arrival."

"Some people say that Grumman makes great airplanes but lousy boats," Connor said. "Anyway, we'll be landing at Newport Airport next, and we'll drive you to your house or the docks to pick up your car, or wherever you want to go."

"Okay," Tony said, refastening his seatbelt. "I guess I can handle ten minutes more."

"Right," Connor said. Then he went back to his seat and started the engines. He water-taxied across the Harbor of Refuge until he could point the nose of the Widgeon into the wind. The engines roared when he opened the throttle, and soon they were flying across the entrance to Narragansett Bay toward Newport.

Lorraine craned her neck to look back into the cabin, where Tony was looking out a window, and she said, "Poor guy. What's he going to do now, without a boat?"

"I'm not worried about that," Connor said. "We'll help him get a new boat. What bothers me is that he might do something about Marco."

"You think he might go after the men who killed his son?" Lorraine said. "After all these years?"

"Exactly," Connor said. "He's running out of time."

Lorraine looked out her side window in silence for a few minutes until she turned and said, "Connor, I have something to tell you."

"If it's about Garcia, I don't want to know," Connor said as he adjusted the throttle levers.

Lorraine went back to looking out the window before she said, "We should make a fresh start, Connor. We'll be empty nesters soon. Are we going to reset our relationship, or—?"

"Right," Connor said. "Maybe it is time to turn our house into your bed-and-breakfast."

"We've been talking about it for years."

"I'll have to quit the airline."

"You'll have this seaplane to play with," Lorraine said. "You might even make a little money flying people out to the islands. And I'd like to quit the newspaper business and finish my novel."

"We'll have to spend a lot of time working together at the house," Connor said. "Is that really what you want?"

"Yes, I do."

"I want that too," Connor said, when he reached between the seats and took her hand. But the moment passed quickly when Connor let go of her fingers and said, "Something is wrong."

He grabbed the yoke and tugged it back to raise the nose and slow their airspeed while standing the Widgeon on one wing to reverse their direction of flight. The horizon spun around and the maneuver happened so rapidly that it took Lorraine a moment to realize they were headed back toward Point Judith.

"What the hell was that?" Lorraine said.

"Sorry, I had to pull an old fighter pilot maneuver there. We don't have a moment to spare."

"You're worried about Bennett and Natalie?"

"Right," Connor said. "It's more like I'm worried that Natalie won't be able to stop Ben from doing something stupid."

Lorraine turned around and saw that Tony was looking toward heaven and crossing himself in the back of the airplane, and she said, "You scared the crap of Tony, too."

"He'll get over it," Connor said. "Tell him to put on a headset so I can talk to him."

Lorraine pointed to the headset that Natalie had worn and pantomimed putting it on her head, which Tony understood. After he put the headset on his head, she said, "Press the microphone close to your lips."

"What happened?" Tony said. "I wasn't expecting any loop-the-loops."

"That was just a steep turn," Connor said. "I needed a quick way to turn around—we're going back to make sure Ben and Natalie are okay."

"Oh, okay," Tony said.

Connor came in low over the narrow inner harbor at Point Judith—the two sides were called Galilee and Jerusalem—and they saw that all the cars and passengers from Block Island were off the *Metacomet* and that the crew was preparing to load for the return trip to the island. There was no sign of Bennett's jeep.

"I'm going around for another pass," Connor said as he began to turn the seaplane to the left.

"Wait a second," Lorraine said. "Isn't that Bennett's jeep going up Point Judith Road?"

"Yeah, that's them," Connor said, after he reversed direction with another sporty turn. "And look who they're following—your rotund little doctor and his creepy driver."

"I'll tell him to back off," Lorraine said as she pulled out her cell phone and tried to dial Bennett's number. But she soon said, "The call won't go through."

"Cell coverage sucks down here," Connor said. "Anyway, sometimes the cell towers just ignore calls from an airplane. We'll just follow them for a few minutes and see what they're up to. With a little luck the doctor will be going to Providence to catch a flight back to Milwaukee."

"Somehow I doubt that," Lorraine said.

Conner climbed a little higher and flew in lazy circles while Bennett and Natalie followed the sidecar motorcycle up the four-lane highway to Tower Hill. When they came to the turnoff for the bridges across Narragansett Bay to Newport, the motorcycle went that way and Bennett followed at a distance.

"That's okay," Lorraine said. "That's where Bennett would normally turn to come home. It could just be a coincidence that the doctor is headed the same way. Maybe his niece or driver—or whatever she is—is taking him to Cape Cod."

"It's my turn to doubt that," Connor said.

"So what do we do?"

"For now, we follow them," Connor said. "But if Bennett goes past Newport, we'll land and call the cops to intercept him before they go any farther."

"I see the jeep and the motorcycle down there," Tony said, with his face pressed against a window. "They're crossing the Jamestown Bridge, both of them."

"Good," Connor said as he also watched them cross the West Passage on the four-lane span. "Let's all keep our eyes on them."

Connor circled a little higher as the jeep and the motorcycle left the bridge that crossed the West Passage and stayed on the highway that cut straight across the wooded acres and pastureland of Conanicut Island, until the pavement took a sweeping turn to the south for the approaches to the giant suspension span of the Newport Bridge.

"Wait a minute," Tony said. "They're not getting on the Newport Bridge."

"What?" Lorraine said. "Where did they go?"

"I've got them," Connor said, after he racked the Widgeon into another steep turn. "They're going to Jamestown."

"I hope the doctor is taking his driver to the Bay Voyage for a bowl of clam chowder," Lorraine said. "Because there's not much else to do in Jamestown this time of year."

"Nope," Tony said. "They went right through Jamestown. Now they're headed to Beavertail Point."

"Ugh," Lorraine said. "It's worse than that—they're turning into Fort Wetherill."

"Damn it," Connor said, looking down at the abandoned bunkers and concrete ramparts of the coastal fortification that had been abandoned after the Second World War. "Ben is letting the doctor lead him straight to an isolated state park. What the hell is that boy thinking?"

"Oh my God," Lorraine said. "You're right. They're following him right into the old fort, and there's nobody else around—except—"

"Nobody except a U-Haul truck," Connor said. "And a beat-up BMW sedan."

They watched from the Widgeon as the motorcycle came to a stop next to the BMW and the rotund form of the doctor dismounted from the sidecar. Then he and his leather-clad driver entered the bunker though the only iron door that was open.

"Those doors were all supposed to be locked or welded shut," Tony said. "Nobody is supposed to go in there—it's a maze of passages and tunnels—and there are holes in the floor that go to the lower levels."

"You've been in there?" Lorraine said.

"Sure," Tony said. "When I was a kid, we used to go all through the old forts in Newport and over here—until the cops caught us."

"Right," Connor said. "But I don't think that Ben will be dumb enough to follow those two weirdoes into a dark labyrinth."

"Guess again," Lorraine said. "Damn it! I'm going to strangle that boy—he's out of the jeep and leading Natalie straight to the door."

"Hang on," Connor said as he racked the Widgeon into a wing-over maneuver to dive down toward the bunker.

"Jesus Mary and Joseph!" Tony said as the earth and sky pivoted outside the cabin windows.

"We're okay," Connor said. "I'm just going to wake those kids up."

He dove down toward the cliffs and pulled up at the last second to pass twenty feet over the top of the bunker with plenty of airspeed and the engines roaring. The airstream whistled around the airframe with a whine like a jet when he pulled up in a sweeping turn.

When he came around far enough to see the teenagers, Connor saw Bennett wave up at him—just before he and Natalie disappeared into the bunker.

"Damn it!" Connor said, smacking the visor above the instrument panel with his hand. Then he pulled the throttles back and banked the wings toward the water in the East Passage as he said, "Make sure your seatbelts are tight."

"What are you going to do?" Lorraine said.

"The only thing we can do—I'm going to land this crate and drag those two out of there."

"You're going to land there?" Lorraine said, pointing to the choppy water in the East Passage.

"No, the ebb tide is working against the wind a little too much out there," Connor said as he cut the engines and lowered the flaps. He turned the Widgeon one more time to face an opening in the rocky cliffs and said, "We'll land in the cove."

"Is there enough room in there?"

"Nope," Connor said. "But if there was ever a time to play against the odds, this is it, so give me room to work. This is going to be a tight one."

When the turn to the shoreline was completed, Lorraine saw that they were facing a narrow cut in the rocky cliffs and that there would be no turning back. The cove ended in a crescent-shaped sandy beach at the bottom of the cliffs.

Connor came across the water low and slow with the nose of the seaplane up, using the power of the engines and a high angle on the wings to fly at the lowest possible airspeed. They were almost into the cove—lower than the rocky slopes on both sides—when a wave reached up and slapped the hull of the Widgeon.

"Crap," Connor said. "Hang on!"

The jolt from below upset the seaplane and nearly started a series of proposing leaps that would have ended with the nose getting stuffed into the water, but Connor goosed the throttle levers to add just enough power to stabilize the wings, and then they were over the calmer water inside the cove.

Connor eased the power to idle as the Widgeon's deep-vee hull settled into the water and spray enveloped the cockpit. Then they heard and felt a hard thump that pushed them rudely forward in their seats.

When the spray cleared, the Widgeon was up on the sandy beach, apparently intact.

"Let's go!" Connor said, as he threw his seatbelt aside and grabbed his .45 from the storage pouch alongside his seat. He rushed to the rear of the cabin and opened the hatch and when Lorraine joined him, they both leaped out onto the sand.

"I'm calling 9-1-1," Lorraine said as they started running uphill toward the bunker.

"No, don't," Connor said. "We don't want a bunch of cops rushing in here with sirens screaming. Not while the kids are in there. We're going to have to get them out ourselves."

"What are we going to do?"

"I'll think of something," Connor said as they scrambled up a rocky slope. "Whatever it takes."

"Wait for me," Tony said.

When Connor looked over his shoulder, he said, "Take it easy, Tony— we've got this." The old seaman was giving all he had to keep up, but his legs were failing him.

"Yeah," Tony said. "Keep going, I'm only slowing you down. You better hurry up!"

Connor and Lorraine struggled up another slope and through a thicket before they came to the concrete courtyard behind the row of bunkers. The rusted steel doors were all shit except for the last one—where the sidecar motorcycle was parked next to a muddy BMW and a U-Haul van.

"Easy now," Connor said, when he stopped Lorraine at the door.

Connor went in first and immediately stepped aside so he would be out of the sunlight coming through the doorway. He found himself in a dank space that smelled like a catacomb, with thick concrete walls, floors, and a ceiling, all splotched with moss and mold. There was another door across the room that led to a passageway.

Their eyes were not fully adjusted to the darkness when Connor and Lorraine started down the passageway, but they soon realized that the junk along the walls on both sides was actually cans and containers that reeked of chemicals.

"What is this place?" Lorraine said.

"My bet is that this old bunker was J.D.'s personal dump," Connor said. "He probably stashed all the toxic waste from the island here for years."

"Oh my God," Lorraine said. "We've got to get the kids out of here right away—this place is full of poison."

"I'm working on it," Connor said. There was faint light coming from an open steel door along the passageway, and Connor stayed close to the wall as he approached it. He used the thick concrete wall as a barricade and leaned just far enough into the doorway to see into the chamber, with his .45 at the ready. What he saw by the light of the one lantern in the center of the space was chilling—piles of electrical transformers and rusty drums and containers of chemicals had been pushed away from the center of the room, where a stack of small wood crates was neatly arranged. The cover was off one of the crates and the gold bars inside glowed in the lantern light. Two bodies—Honey and Dirk—were near the crates of treasure, where they had oozed a large pool of blood onto the floor.

Herman and his "niece"—now *sans* wig and obviously a man—were behind the gold holding Natalie and Bennett, with pistols pressed to their heads.

Bennett squirmed to get free of the leather-clad man and he said, "Dad, get this creep off me!"

"Don't move, Ben," Connor said, using the doorframe as a barricade and training his sights on the tall man's shaved head.

"That's far enough," Herman said. "Too far, in fact. But if you toss your gun on the floor and come in here, I'll let these two loose."

"Then what?" Connor said.

"We will lock you and your children in one of these rooms while Michael and I load the gold aboard the U-Haul," Herman said. "The police will come looking for you after they spot your seaplane in the cove."

"That's a stupid idea," Connor said. "That way you will finish us and still take our children as hostages."

The thought of hostages seemed to appeal to Michael—*nee* Michelle—and he smiled and tugged Bennett tightly against his leathers.

"Natalie," Lorraine said, talking from behind Connor. "Are you okay, sweetheart?"

"Yes. I'm just afraid."

"We're okay," Bennett said. "This big guy just smells bad, that's all."

"We're going to get you out of here," Lorraine said as she showed herself for a moment and moved to the opposite side of the doorway, where she could also lean in and see the teenagers.

"The only way is to do as I say," Herman said.

"There is always another way," Lorraine said. "Let's just take it slow and figure out how we can all get what we want."

"Don't try to fool me," Herman said. "I'm immune to a woman's sweet talking. Your husband will have to make up his mind."

"I don't know about that," Connor said. He knew himself well enough to realize that he only had one approach to problems—a full-on frontal assault—while Lorraine was the master of compromise. "You might want to listen to her, Doctor. Maybe we can all get what we need out of this mess."

"Exactly," Lorraine said. "One thing I'm wondering about is how you knew all this gold was in here?"

"I'm not a fool," Herman said. "I know what you're trying to do."

"Then there's no harm in humoring me, Doctor," Lorraine said. "I know you had to be smart to figure this out before the rest of us."

"If you must know," Herman said as his ego took over. "I approached Logan with a proposition. I knew that he was short of ready cash and that he could not dispose of over thirty million dollars of gold bullion without the services of a certain kind of broker. So, I offered him one hundred thousand dollars in good faith money for the exclusive rights to offer this commodity on the underground gold exchange, at a five percent commission. He leapt at the offer, of course, while insisting that I pass the cash to him here, while everyone was distracted by the discovery on the U-853."

"Why don't you just call it the black market?" Connor said. "And you must have known they were going to kill you as soon as you showed up here with that much cash."

"Again, I'm no fool," Herman said, pointing to the corpses on the floor. "It occurred to me that Logan would not have told these two that I would be coming for a share of the gold. So as soon as he was in custody, I knew I could make my move."

"Which brings us back to the nub," Lorraine said. "How do we each get what we want?"

"I couldn't care less about that gold," Connor said. "I'll never surrender my sidearm and I'm not leaving until those kids are on my side of this door. So you'd better think real hard about your next move."

"There it is," Lorraine said. "The solution is clear—I'll come in as your hostage and you can let the children go. Connor will take them outside and he won't call the police until long after we leave with the gold. You can leave me somewhere on the side of the road."

"That's a deal," Connor said. "We don't give a damn about the gold—or Dirk and Honey—we just want to get those kids home in one piece."

Herman said, "I don't know—"

Take the deal, Connor thought. *All I need is a clear shot when you let go of those kids. Take the damn deal!*

That was when Connor heard a minor commotion behind his back as Tony came stomping down the passage, breathing heavily.

"What's this bullshit about hostages?" Tony said. Then as soon as he reached the doorway and saw the tableau in the light of the lantern, he said, "What the fuck is this?" He was stomping into the room and charging at Michael like a hobbled bull when he said, "Hey, you dickhead, you want to hold a gun on somebody? Try it on me, asshole!"

Michael panicked and loosened his grip on Bennett when he raised his pistol to Tony. His first shot hit Tony in the leg—he went down right away—but his second went wild and ricocheted off the concrete ceiling when Bennett pushed his arm up. Then the teenager jumped aside to help Natalie, which left the tall man in leathers wide open, with his eyes wide and his jaw dropped.

Connor fired with his sights zeroed in at the center of Michael's chest and felt his .45 give a satisfying kickback. He had learned long ago that the secret of getting the pistol back on the target was all in the wrist, and he pushed the muzzle down as he was aiming for his second shot, which went slightly lower, into the diaphragm.

Bennett tackled Natalie out of Herman's grasp, which stunned the rotund little man. He looked at Michael dead or dying on the floor and gave out a sound that none of the living in that bunker would ever forget—something between a gasp and a banshee's screech—and he raised his pistol to Connor.

It's something to see a man's resolve hardening, his face going from shock to anger. That's what Conner read in Herman's countenance as he fired his .45 four times in rapid succession—Herman had to be dead before he hit the floor since he would land almost on top of Bennett and Natalie—and the rotund man knocked over the lamp as he fell. Then the echoes of Connor's shots reverberated down the hall and back to their ears until there was sudden stillness and silence in the now flickering light.

"Tony!" Bennett said, as he jumped up and went to the old seadog, who was rolling and cursing on the floor.

Connor stepped closer with his .45 ready to finish his work. The lantern was on the floor, flickering between Honey and Dirk—who were definitely dead—as was the rotund man, with most of his face left of his nose gone and the other eye open—with the eyeball rolled up into a death stare at the ceiling. Michael was unconscious and dying—a corpse taking its final labored, gasping breaths—after being hit twice in the kill zone by full metal jacket slugs from Connor's .45 automatic.

"Get the kids out of here," Connor said to Lorraine. "Call 9-1-1, and go to the road and guide the cops to this bunker. And for the love of God, tell them that the shooting is all over so they don't get trigger happy when they come in here."

"Right," Lorraine said as she grabbed Natalie by the arm.

"I won't leave Tony," Bennett said.

"Get the hell out of here, kid!" Tony said. "This ain't the first time a bullet found me, for Christ's sake."

Then Lorraine pulled Bennett and Natalie out of the bunker into the sunlight.

"Hold some pressure on that wound," Connor said as he put his .45 on the floor and stepped away from it. "I'm going to have to stand in the doorway with my hands up when the cops arrive—they're going to freak out when they see this mess."

Before Conner turned for the door, he took a moment to stand alongside Tony and gaze at the pile of cursed gold and toxic waste in a dank bunker lit by the flickering light of the toppled lantern, strewn with grotesquely mutilated corpses.

Goddamn," Tony said, when he sat up to take a look. "What a sight. Goddamn them to hell—every one of them."

"Right," Connor said. "They chose their own fate—don't we all?"

THE END

Author's Note

This story is the third book of a series which I call *Connor Laird—
Airman's Adventures*. Like the first two volumes, which play off state-
sponsored drug smuggling from Cuba to Florida, this tale also dances
on the fault line between fact and fiction. It is a fact that to this day the
wreck of the U-853 lies upright and broken by bombs and depth
charges in the shallow waters of Rhode Island Sound, but legends of
Nazi gold bullion aboard this or any other sunken U-boat are clearly
fantasy.

It is also an historical fact that Nazi saboteurs landed from U-boats
in Amagansett, New York, and near Jacksonville, Florida, in 1942 and
again on the Maine coast in 1944. These spies were all captured (as far
as we know) and executed or imprisoned by military tribunals. Any
suggestion that a mysterious provocateur landed on Block Island in the
closing hours of WWII is solely a product of my imagination and exists
only on these pages.

Since the Kriegsmarine gave their U-boats numbers but not names,
the actual crew of the U-853 gave their boat the unofficial nickname of
The Tightrope Walker, which I appropriated as Rusty Drake's name for
the mystery man who came in from the sea—it was simply too good a
fit to pass up. Likewise, the name of Tony's boat was borrowed from the
trawler *F/V Racketeer*, which fished from Point Judith for many years.

Some readers will also note that the coal ship *Marine Electric*, which
crosses the *Racketeer*'s bow in Chapter 7, was actually lost at sea in
February 1983, decades before the era of this story; that there was no
continuous newspaper on Block Island until the *Block Island Times* was
founded in 1970; and that landing a Grumman amphibious airplane in

salt water is highly inadvisable due to corrosion and structural problems (see *Chalk Ocean Airways Flight 101*). I apologize to those who may be offended by these "mistakes" and others—it is fiction, after all.

The name of Laura Houghtaling Ingalls (not to be confused with the writer Laura Ingalls Wilder) is used here fictitiously and as far as I know she never visited Block Island, nor is there any connection to the U-853. However, it is an historical fact that Houghtaling Ingalls was the first person to be convicted under the Foreign Agents Registration Act (FARA) which is much in the news these days.

As for Connor Laird's low opinion of Nazi sympathizers in America no apology is forthcoming. The German-American Bund and the America First Committee were among the most shameful episodes of anti-Semitism and xenophobia in our past. May I suggest that it is not enough to say *never forget*—we must *never forget that it could happen here*, as early as tomorrow.

In writing this book I am indebted to my friend Michael J. Maynard who served with me at the Point Judith Coast Guard Station back in the day. Mike knows more about the early history of the US Coast Guard and the US Life Saving Service than anyone I have ever met and it was he who suggested that I should tell this story—sort of. Mike pitched the tale of a son who goes searching for the lost gold that his father saw Nazis bury on Misquamicut Beach in WWII—which was a story of cowardice, remorse, and hope that I could not write. However, he was very helpful in developing the character of Cole Lonsdale, whose name derives from two streets in Pawtucket, Rhode Island.

This book was a departure from the first two volumes of Connor Laird's adventures and the story told in *Whom Fortune Favors* and *Fate of the Bold* is not yet complete. Our heroes—sadly minus Rene Garcia—have more work to do in the shadow of Popocatepetl, the active volcano in Mexico where the fates of *la bandida* Leona and the artist Pilar Vasquez are yet to be determined. I can only hope that reading these stories of Connor and Lorraine, Bennett and Nathan, Ali Vasquez and the rest of this crew will be as enjoyable as the writing has been for me.

Finally, a teaser—the four gold bars that were on the deck of the *Racketeer* would not have been destroyed by the underwater explosion.

Rather, they are resting on the bottom of Rhode Island Sound a short distance from what is left of the U-853—which is a fact known only to Tony and Connor.

Happy reading!

Doug Cooper
Bristol, Rhode Island, USA

www.dscooperbooks.com

Made in the USA
Middletown, DE
12 December 2019

The search for a missing surfer draws Connor and Lorraine Laird into the mystery of a sunken U-boat and a Nazi saboteur who was killed on Block Island in the closing hours of World War II.

DOUGLAS S. COOPER is a former US Coast Guard chief warrant officer, professional mariner and deep sea diver. He is also a licensed comercial pilot who has authored eight books since he began writing in 2012 while recovering from a serious flying accident. Doug lives in Bristol, Rhode Island USA.

ISBN 978-0-9984100-5-0

Design by EbookLaunch.com
Images from Shutterstock
Widgeon Leaving the Northport Fly-in by Jim Sorbie